Francis Saltus Saltus

Honey and Gall

Poems

Francis Saltus Saltus

Honey and Gall
Poems

ISBN/EAN: 9783743324343

Manufactured in Europe, USA, Canada, Australia, Japa

Cover: Foto ©Andreas Hilbeck / pixelio.de

Manufactured and distributed by brebook publishing software
(www.brebook.com)

Francis Saltus Saltus

Honey and Gall

HONEY AND GALL.

POEMS.

BY

FRANCIS S. SALTUS.

PHILADELPHIA:
J. B. LIPPINCOTT & CO.
1873.

Je suis comme le roi d'un pays pluvieux,
Riche, mais impuissant, jeune et pourtant très-vieux,
Qui, de ses précepteurs méprisant les courbettes,
S'ennuie avec ses chiens comme avec d'autres bêtes.
Rien ne peut l'égayer, ni gibier, ni faucon,
Ni son peuple mourant en face du balcon.
Du bouffon favori la grotesque ballade
Ne distrait plus le front de ce cruel malade ;
Son lit fleurdelisé se transforme en tombeau,
Et les dames d'atour, pour qui tout prince est beau,
Ne savent plus trouver d'impudique toilette
Pour tirer un souris de ce jeune squelette.
Le savant qui lui fait de l'or n'a jamais pu
De son être extirper l'élément corrompu,
Et dans ces bains de sang qui des Romains nous viennent,
Et dont sur leurs vieux jours les puissants se souviennent,
Il n'a su réchauffer ce cadavre hébété
Où coule au lieu de sang, l'eau verte du Léthé.

BAUDELAIRE.

CONTENTS.

5

PROEM.

THIS, the song of my blood and the singing—
    Of pains, I now offer to please.
What I bring in the seed is the bringing
    Of fruits that will ripen and ease
Bitter thoughts, by a perfume close clinging,
    By these rhyme-storms, like turbulent seas.

I sing of strange songs and the wringing
    Of hands in fatidical zeal,—
Of great gloom-throated bells, ever ringing
    With wild poems of bronze till they reel.
I sing of all terrors hell-springing,
    And I sing of our woe and our weal.

Like a bee on a tulip-leaf swinging,
    I extract all the juice and the meat,
All the dross and the dew, nothing flinging—
    Aside, whether good or effete.
For are bees to be shunned for their stinging,
    If their honey is luscious and sweet?

THE OWL.

AN ebon night had masked the sky,
Great hueless clouds soared grimly by,
They seemed to moan, they seemed to sigh—
    With sullen ire.
For, in a dream, I sought the gloom
Of shadows, light as downy plume,
Urging me to an awful doom
    Of flame and fire.

O'er jaggèd thorny burs I sped,
Coiled vipers' fangs with poison bled,
Filling my anxious soul with dread,
    Vast-eyed, supreme.
While sinking deep in boggy sod
My feet on spotted toadlets trod,
As at a frantic pace I plod,
    Still in a dream.

Methought a grassy mound I spied ;
But no ! my sunken eyes had lied ;
For baffled, on the ground I cried
    In vain for help.
A gummy dew oozed from an oak
Where hideous frogs, with brazen croak,
Hell-elfs and gnomes, their ghouls invoke
    With yaup and yelp.

My seething brain could find no rest,
Consumed by ardent fiery zest;
Like scorpion sting, like Orient pest,
  Raved I as wild.
Till heaven recalled its meekest boon,
And through the glade an opal moon,
With oafish glee—round-facèd loon!—
  Wickedly smiled.

From foxy stench, from leafy glen,
From musty acorn, gluish fen,
From fulvid badgers' tainted den,
  I wildly fled;
While ghastly, yexing birds of prey,
Huge, crested vultures, death-fowls gray,
Who hell and Satan still obey,
  Whirred o'er my head.

Why do I tremble? why that stare?
Do you not see it gazing there,
Silently waiting for its share
  Of sinning blood?
An Owl, with oval, lurid eye,
Utt'ring its solemn, dismal cry,
Warning me that I came to die
  In fecal mud!

Yes! 'tis an owl, with ashy plume,
Whose fretful beak begins to fume
For bodies from a fresh-dug tomb,
  To swell its feast!

To warp and mangle flesh and bone,
Whether of harlot, king, or crone,
Till thirsty lust for blood alone
  Had ever ceased.

I saw it leer, I saw it grin,
It hooted me for every sin,
And whizzed about with horrid din,
  From tree to tree.
Its gleaming eyes began to gloat,
Its venomed claws sank in my throat,
Forced me, by fetid breath, to bloat—
  With agony !

The night-fiend held me in its clasp,
And stung and sucked like amber asp,
While in its damp and putrid grasp
  My life-veins bled !
It rustled like a tocsin knell,
Its mournful whine and withering smell
Was like a demon's, deep in hell,
  Shuddering of dread !

The nauseous bird had clutched me fast ;
Another second was my last,
Had I not round its necklet ghast
  Pressed my mad nails.
With reeking mouth I bit its jowl,
Till half the hairy-facèd fowl
Sank in the mire with fright-toned howl
  And human wails !

* * * * * * *

2*

On waking from this odious dream
I saw the bright sun gently gleam,
With many a golden, dazzling beam,
    Upon the floor.
Weary, oppressed, with sleep replete,
I rose the morning rays to greet,
But fainted ; for my hands and feet
    Were red with gore !

SPIRITS OF SIN.

GLANCE with the vivid azure of thine eyes,
   O'erarched by curving brows of glossy jet,
Down on my lips, still roscid with the prize
   They captured from thy fragrant coral wet.
      Flash like a steel blade tipped with fire,
        Flash with thy luxuries of light ;
      Into my soul's gloom let thy gaze
        Bathe, till grown dizzy by the sight,
Sin's spirits shroud in mantles of delight
Our ardent ken in one delirious daze.

Fast on thy shoulders, rounded, fleecy pure,
   Sting the hot kisses thou wouldst check in vain ;
Looped on those charms that would a saint allure,
   Soft will I lie, till happiness is pain.
      Then will thy drooping lash of silk
        Hide thy eyes' else too potent gleam ;

Then will the splendors of thy gaze
 Pierce deeper in thy joy supreme.
Sin's spirits hover while we fondly dream,
And gently o'er our heads their gray wings raise.

So on through life; ecstatic moments sweet,
 No godlier gift ask I when by thee warmed
Each burning face can a more burning meet,
 So suavely rapt, and by each other charmed.
  So let us live until the force
   Of youth is drained from inner core,
  Long sleepless nights, long languid days,
   Till by loved surfeit all is o'er.
Sin's spirits then will guard us evermore,
To prove that our sweet life was one of praise.

PANTHEISM.

DESPITE the priest, despite the sage,
 Despite the lore of eld,
I feel that in a by-gone age
Our souls, by an almighty mage,
 Were in strange prisons held.

I feel that love was not unknown
 To mute and silent things:
That ardor lurked within a stone,
That marble felt each varied tone,
 The scale of passion sings.

In that suave age of tranquil days
    When everything was soul,
The amorous sun with golden blaze
Showered down on earth its glorious rays,
    Flooding it pole to pole.

The brooklet bubbled o'er with love
    For rushes on its edge :
Perched on an oak-tree's bough above,
A mottled queest and tender dove
    Exchanged their cooing pledge.

Each star and cloud, each leaf and flower,
    Each grass-blade steeped in dew,
By unknown gods received as dower
The will, the sense, the nerve, and power
    To love as mortals do.

Pearl, coral, jasper, gold, and sand,
    Gems hued in glitt'ring grace,
Obeyed the great Creator's hand,
And lived and loved in every land,
    Smiling before his face.

But years and time bring on decay,
    Fair gems no longer sigh ;
Both flowers and rushes fade away,—
Vermine and rust command their prey,
    And marble love must die.

Metamorphosis strange and sweet !
    Wondrous yet solemn death !

The essences of dead loves meet,—
To bud anew *our* souls to greet
   With fresh and virile breath.

While all an unknown world of bliss,
   A universe of soul !
Revives beneath kind nature's kiss
And lives another life in this,
   With pleasure as a goal.

Thou whom I love,—thy love was known
   In that fair age gone by :
Was it the love of gem or stone ?
Was it the love of waves alone ?
   Was it the zephyr's sigh ?

Those radiant orbs my senses prize,
   Six thousand years ago,
Shone as twin-stars in vaulted skies,
Then fell to earth to form thine eyes,
   Thine eyes of opal glow.

'Neath Ceylon's reefs, a coral bed,
   Six thousand years ago,
Detached by billows as they sped,
Has formed thy lips of ruddy red
   By changes strange and slow.

A bunch of pearlets 'neath the tide,
   Six thousand years ago,
Was moulded when its spirit died
To form thy teeth, thy nacker pride,
   Those teeth thou lov'st to show.

Aroused from out a crumbling rest
   Six thousand years ago,
The granite's love again is blessed,
By breathing in thy virgin breast,—
   That breast as white as snow.

I feel secure that far in space,
   Six thousand years ago,
I saw and loved a cherub face.—
I died, alas! and lost the trace,
   But found it here below.

Descending from another sphere,
   Six thousand years ago,
Perhaps I loved thee *there* as *here;*
In which world was my love most dear?—
   Thy soul alone can know!

PERFUMES.

PERFUMES, like sounds and colors, lend
   A subtle charm to art:
Their mystic fragrances can blend
   With occult thrills of heart;
   While odorous fumes ascend,
   Fixed soulward, and impart
   A sweetness to befriend
   The noisome smart
Of spleen, or sorrows that contend.

Santal recalleth pomp and gold,
Luxurious dreams superb !
Festivals, pageants manifold,—
Wines, revelries, disturb.
Purple, and gems of mould
A mind wealth-dazzled, curb—
By spendent scenes untold,
While loud reverb
The dance-bells, mellow, silver-souled.

Rose-attar to the nostril brings
Balm, tranquilness, and peace ;
A sky, blue, musing, moves and swings
Its clouds like snow-laved fleece.
A smell of virgin wings,
A smell of vales in Greece,
Pervades the sense and stings,
Till sweet surcease
Is craved, to dream of other things.

Benzoin brings fumes of mordant lust,
Wild, tempting vapors seethe !
Houris' flusht nipples craze the gust :
Their breaths are hot to breathe.
Supple-formed nymphs robust,
Lascive, nard-bathed, bequeath—
Vague, fleshy scents with trust,
Sheathe and unsheathe
Sword-tongues, imperious of thrust !

Incense, myrrh-redolent, conveys
A temple's grandeur, stern :
An unctuous voice chants cloistral lays,
The censers' perfumes burn,

A holy, bluish blaze.
Iron bells have chimed nocturn ;
    The sins of nights and days
        All minds concern,
Tears contrite mix with tears of praise !

Musk, vistas tropical can paint,
        Its sweet recalls the breeze
Of Cuba's hills : aromas faint
    Spring, zephyr-toucht, to ease
        Of listlessness the plaint.
    Blue gleen the distant seas,
        Blue as the eyes of saint,
            While over lees
Gush scents of unknown savor quaint.

Others, far subtler, can excite,
        Though ownerless of name.
Such are the essences of light,—
    The perfumes of a flame,
        The smell of first snow, white,
    Some picture's olden frame.
        But sweeter far by night
            Dead kisses claim,
Though passed, an od'rous vague delight.

OBLIVION.

WHEN drunk with gore the foeman spurs
 His maddened charger o'er a field
 Where gashèd, mangled corpses yield—
Beneath the iron-shod Death that errs,
And in its fury opes and stirs
 Deep wounds with clotted blood half sealed.
  Some men may weep,
   And others laugh ;
  I neither laugh nor weep,
   But quaff—
 My wine, and find repose in sleep.

When chill with rage the tempest drives
 The scudding hell-doomed ship to sea,
 And strident, shrieks in blast of glee
With raucous voice, that sobs for lives,
And taunteth when the vessel strives
 To shun its fate, or flee the lee,
  Some men may weep,
   And others laugh ;
  I neither laugh nor weep,
   But quaff—
 My wine, and find repose in sleep.

When mortals find that all is naught,
 That life is but one vast decoy,—
 False in its pain, more false in joy,

Rotten in action and in thought;
And when they learn—with wisdom fraught—
   That time can ev'ry trust destroy,
     Some men may weep,
      And others laugh;
     I neither laugh nor weep,
      But quaff—
     My wine, and find repose in sleep.

BARCELONA, January, 1873.

LACQUER-WORK.

THE city I love is in Japan,
With streets spread out like a lady's fan;
High towers of porcelain, white and blue,
O'ertop the cottages of bamboo.
Pagodas lacquered enchant my eye,
Their kaolin steeples pierce the sky.
Rare birds, with plumage all gold and red,
Chirp sweetest melodies o'er my head.
Strange idols, carvèd, of costume quaint,
Grin blandly on me from out their paint.
A music, not sad, yet dreamy, swells:
Its rhythm keeps time with silv'ry bells.
*   *   *   *   *   *   *   *
My lovely idol is hidden here,
With inch-long eyes and a gaze sincere;
Her feet are so small she cannot walk,
Her breast is as white as snow or chalk;
Her laugh is like sunshine, full of glee,
And her sweet breath smells like fresh-made tea. .

STANZAS.

On a dark long December night,
    I delight
To gaze upon some church, robed white—
  With snow ; its steeples capped with rime.
And in the cemetery near,
    Chill and drear,
I love to see the dying year—
  Struggle against resistless time.

I love to hear the ice-blast bleak
    Moan and shriek
Over the grave-yard's cedars, weak—
  And bending 'neath its storm-mad kiss :
And as I sit to watch it lift
    Each snow-drift,
While scattering ev'ry flake, and rift
  The trembling tombstones by its hiss.

Here seek I peace, for memories blend,
    And a friend,
The only one I own, can lend—
  A surcease to my grief below ;
For I have suffered, loved, and pined,
    And I find
In tempest's voices, rough, unkind,
  A sympathizer for my woe.

Vittoria, December, 1872.

THE SKELETON SEXTON.

A RHENISH legend, quaint and drear,
   Told in a mystic uncouth rhyme,
By chance fell on my awe-struck ear,—
A tale of horror and of fear,
   Strange echo of an olden time;
      For it sang of a bell,
      A rusty bell,
        Which hung
        And rung
        With brazen tongue
      From a church in a lonely dell.

The steeple of the haunted kirk
   O'erlooked the graves of buried dead,
Where phantoms pale were known to lurk
Silently 'neath the garish smirk
   Of chilly moonbeams overhead;
      And they gazed at that bell,
      That heavy bell,
        Which hung
        And rung
        With brazen tongue
      From the church in the lonely dell.

At stroke of midnight there appeared,
   From out the shadows dense and gray,
A skeleton of aspect weird,
Who paused and at the tombstones leered,

Then to the belfry sped his way ;
   And he tolled that bell,
   That drowsy bell,
     Which hung
     And rung
     With brazen tongue
From the church in the lonely dell.

Around his bones he wraps a shroud,
   And rings till kirk and cloister shake,
While other eager spirits crowd
And laugh so shrill, and laugh so loud,
   That seems as if the dead would wake ;
     For at every knell
     Of that rusty bell,
      Which hung
      And rung
      With brazen tongue
     Some mortal fell
     In the depths of hell.

*   *   *   *   *

Now, when I hear at midnight hour
   A sad and solemn funeral dirge,
Even in dreams, I bend and cower,
Shrinking aghast from occult power
   And shadows grim which forth emerge ;
     And I think of that bell,
     That mellow bell,
      Which hung
      And rung
      With brazen tongue
From the church in the lonely dell.

3*

This is the legend, quaint and drear,
  Told in a mystic uncouth rhyme,
Which fell upon my awe-struck ear,—
A tale of wonder and of fear,
  Strange echo of an olden time.

———————

TO ——.

FAIR Creole, lava-moulden,
  Warm are thy Cuban skies;
Warm is thy sun and golden,
  But warmer are thine eyes,—
    Twin suns of jet,
    My life's sole prize.

Fair Creole, all thy kissings
  Are unctuous as oil;
Low are thy sultry hissings
  When eager thou dost toil,
    And round my neck
    Tanned arms dost coil.

Fair Creole, the sweet savor
  Of thy hot breath's perfume,
As o'er thy lips I quaver,
  And all thy soul consume,
    With avid clutch
    Will haste my doom.

Fair Creole, though the frailest,
   Art forged of iron and steel,
My lacks of love bewailest,
   When I before thee kneel;
     That love hast killed
     By thoughtless zeal.

Fair Creole, thou hast lavished
   Youth, beauty, charm, sincere—
But I, by passions ravished,
   Have given more, I fear:
     My life and blood,
     Lost tear by tear.

GOYA.*

THY bitter brush was lightning-tipped,
     And dipped
In blacks of night, in golds of day;
   The violent nightmares of thy whim,
     Pain-dim,
Were wont in hideous worlds to stray,
   In troubled seas of fright to swim.

Thine hues, betinged with tears of gall,
     Recall
The horrors of the Schwarzwald's eves;
   The mystery of eerie skies
     Low, plies
Over thy canvass, moans and grieves
   A ghastly music, born of sighs.

* A celebrated Spanish painter and caricaturist. Died 1828.

Behold the tint of clouds that swoon !
   The moon
Leers on a fishless, phantom lake ;
  Gaunt, threatening shadows hellward loom.
   The gloom
Chills the damned glance of fiends who slake
  Their thirsts with mud, whom fires consume.

Ever the nacarat gleams of fire,
   Red, dire,
Light the wild wonders of thy work ;
  Visions that pall, with colors cursed,
   Now burst
On riven gaze, or lie and lurk,
  The last more harrowing than the first !

Yet in thy better, happier hours,
   Fair flowers,
Fruits, and queen-bodied virgins smile—
  From out a golden florid paint,
   Dream-faint
Chimeras, born to calm awhile
  The terrors of thy ceaseless plaint.

Thy dark-orbed sirens of Seville
   Can thrill:
The majos' velvet jacket gleams ;
  Or, from Granada's sculptured halls,
   There falls
The soft, pale light of marble dreams :
  Thy dormant Muse forgets her galls.

See there again the plaza full !
   The bull

Swelters in foaming sweat and gore;
  The echo of ten thousand throats,
    Parched, dotes
Over the dying beast. Strife-sore,
  A people every quiver notes.

We see the grand and brutal fun,
    The sun
Pouring its rays on eager girls,
  Slow-eyed, who beg th' espada's skill
    To kill;
But torture first the bull in furls—
  Of silk, before his blood turns still.

Colorful glories of old Spain,
    Long lain
For ages in the glooms of time,
  Thou hast revived with potent brush,
    The flush
Of all that golden, glorious clime,
  With tintings masterful and lush.

Some sad, vague, cloistral solitude,
    As viewed
By mutinous moonbeams, greeting clouds,
  Shows sights our modern fancies shun :
    A nun,—
Robed in long, white, cross-streakèd shrouds,
  Waiting till vesper mass be done.

She steals without in gardens dark,
    The spark—

Of watching eyes directs her feet ;
  Her chaplet's beads 'neath cowl of monk,
    Love-drunk.
Are kisst upon her bosom's sweet,
  A fragile form in sin has sunk.—

The shivering shadows of the rack,
    Dark, black,
Loom on thy canvass, where, in fear,
  Some pallid sufferer is dragged,
    Iron-gagged,
Through corridors, dank, humid, drear,
  With jaggèd stone, dirt-mingled, flagged.

The venoms of thy musings foul
    Oft scowl
Savagely from their colored cloaks.
  Like Ribera, thy genius rare—
    Of prayer,
The myths of noisome thought invokes,
  For what was vile thou madest fair.

Great dreamer ! let thy sleep be light.
    The bright
Aurora of reviving art
  Will warm thy soul's forsaken rest.
    Thou, blest
With gems of fancy and of heart,
  Wilt live in Spain among the best !

MADRID, December, 1872.

DREAM OF ICE.

Oh, wondrous, solemn mystery of Dream !
   Sublime induction of a formless thought—
How vivid is thy cloud-constructed theme !
   Divine of fancy, and by mind unsought,
   Marvel of color, nameless and untaught,
Appalling glimpses of a world supreme !

I saw in sleep, with thrills of proud delight,
   Vistas of algid spheres, and such a view
As never yet of man had blurred the sight,
   Which none can tell of, or conceive of few.—
   In planets far, through billion leagues of blue,
A vision of an airless city, white.

Mammoth cathedrals, higher than the eye
   Could reach ; of architecture hybrid, weird,
Their slender steeples through a freezing sky,
   With grand, stupendous gracefulness upreared.
   Palaces, portals, monuments appeared,
And endless avenues rolled in and by. . . . . . .

Titanic domes on massive temples rose,
   Like a young giant virgin's niveous breast,
Chilling, soul-thrilling in their stern repose,
   As if defying gods, by gods unblest ;
   While pillars, columns, worked of plinth and
       crest,
Upheld the mass with firmest strength, rugose.

And all was ice and all was white; no air,
  No earth, no flame; all frigid, rigid cold!
An icen labyrinth of grand despair.
  The sad necropolis of a race now old,
  Damned for anterior sinnings manifold
By one chill glance of God's avenging stare!

The trees of solid ice had leaves of snow;
  Huge, pendent icicles from heights unseen
Twisted in uncouth shapes, while to and fro
  Swung skies of silver frost, steel-color, keen,
  Superbly monotone of phantom gleen,
Veiling a pallid moon's blear, brumal glow!

Long lines of statues guarded every street,
  With cloaks of rime, with trailing beards of
        hail,
Frigidly gazing, with blank eyes discreet,
  From rough and icy socles, mute and pale,
  Waiting to tell their agonizing tale,
Waiting some sympathizing face to greet.

And all was still: a silence kin to pain,
  And desolate as death, sad, vague, austere,
Save when the echo of some spirit-strain
  Murmured half-frozen melodies of fear. . . . .
  The ghastly moon would pause and disappear
Through hueless heavens, and would come again.—

Oh, 'twas a grand and mighty dream of ice!
  A poem of white snows: sublimest grave,
Whose very dreariness would souls entice,—

Souls flusht and sick of terrene heats, who, brave
Would eagerly renounce our God, and crave
A tomb in this pale, peerless paradise !

And I had seen it all, my spirit paced
   Those broad, bleak thoroughfares of gray and
      white.
No air had I to breathe ; my lungs were braced
   With belts of freezing vapor, fresh and light ;
   And, as I wandered on from site to site,
My thoughts of fire this mortal chill effaced.

For well do I recall my dream, and see
   The strange, fantastic town of ice and rime ;
I still discern each palace, porch, and tree
   That reared its splendor in this boreal clime ;
   And I remember how, from time to time,
I strove to cool my maddening love for thee. . . .

S L E E P.

SUBTLE softness soulward stealing,
   Sleep ! sweet savior still sincere.
Silent, soothing, sorrow-sealing,
   Sombre shadow, sad, severe !

SPLEEN.

The nurse of my childhood was Pain,
　And my infant lips reveled and drank
From bare bosoms, consoling, humane,
　Milk sourer than hatreds, and rank,
　　Till they dried by the drain,
　　Till they withered and shrank.

And the foam of that milk's gangrene
　Was like oils to my parchèd tongue;
For right docile was I to wean
　As helpless my bodilet hung,
　　Sucking pains that were keen,—
　　Sucking pains till they stung!

When thè torrent had ebbed in tide,
　The kindly, cold nipples I tore—
Into shreds, as I puled, and I cried
　Over flesh that was bleeding and sore,
　　For more Pain from that side,
　　For more Pain, and still more.

For the pleasures and joys of Pain
　Are as welcome, refreshing, and fresh
As the deluge of early spring rain,
　As the large-weighted drops to the flesh—
　　Of all kine, by murrain
　　Left skin-tender and nesh.

But I found no more Pain, while Spleen,
　　With its pale and its yellow leer,
With its infamous touch venene,
　　With its pitiless brutal sneer,
　　　With its milt and its teen,
　　Came to blight my career.

A mantle of sinister gloom
　　Has made night of my light and day,
My vindictive thoughts shift and loom,
　　Vague fancies of Fear and Dismay,
　　　While the spleens of the tomb
　　Suck my heart's blood away.

PROFILE.

HALF of a face love I, superbly Greek!
　　The other half ignore, and would not know
Its charms or its deceits; why should I seek
　　The fair uncertainties that sight might show,
When to mine eyes a perfect profile, sleek
　　And softly languorous of artistic flow,
Smileth in splendid curves from front to cheek,
　　Rubied between by lips of luscious glow?
No! in rapt contemplation I prefer
　　To gaze upon its Nauplian mould, and stir
My chaos of mad musings to revere
　　The peerless purity of such a face;
For God had sculptured from an angel's tear
　　This pale, proud profile of sublimest grace!

ESCURIAL.

GRAND sepulchre of royal hates, dank grave
  Of bitter thoughts morose, of cares and spleens,
Cyclops of granite, where at midnight rave
  Through gelid crypts the souls of kings and queens,
What art thou in thy dismal desert, save—
  The silent phantom of Spain's by-gone scenes?
Does not grim Philip's spirit haunt the naves
  Of thy stern cloisters with his mind's gangrenes?
Oh, walls of groans! oh, blood-hewn aisles and domes!
  A sad, drear monotone of echoes roams
From Guadarramian heights around thy gloom,
  The frozen prayers of Torquemada's slain!
Cursed be thy silence, monstrous, chilly tomb!
  Crumble and rot, gray fiend of stone and pain!

THE FACE IN THE FIRE.

I CANNOT sit before a fire
  And warm my shivering limbs:
The candent sparks my senses tire,
For a wild vision grim and dire
  My eye with terror dims.

And every dazzling, flickering flame
  Darting from out the coal,

Stirs up a fierce immortal shame,
To seethe and simmer through my frame
   And agonize my soul.

I cannot stand its withering light,
   Its hot and horrid glare :
My heart shrinks back in awed affright,
I close my eyes to mask a sight
   That fills me with despair.

And cruel memories flit by,
   Sad memories of the past ;
I drop my weary head, and sigh,—
And though to check the tears I try,
   They will fall thick and fast.

For when I raise my eyes to peep
   Into the fire again,
I feel the cold sweat o'er me creep,
My burning pulses throb and leap
   In misery of pain !

Alas ! can ever I be free
   From that strange demon face,
Gazing from out the flames at me,
Haunting me with satanic glee,
   Which no power can efface ?

Once it was living, meek and bland :
   In Hades now 'tis sunk ;
I sent it there with my own hand,
I thrust it down to Stygian strand,
   One night by passion drunk !

4*

The face was of a peerless maid,
  But she was faithless found :
Her oath and marriage vows betrayed;
And so I seized my nitid blade
  And smote her to the ground !

Beneath my jealous glance she bent,
  And from her bleeding side
Her false and perjured heart I rent,
And with a brutal blow I sent
  To fiends the tongue that lied !

For no sad proof did I inquire,
  But, by my rage possessed,
In fiercest frenzy of my ire,
I hurled her body in the fire
  With stern and savage zest !

And now her face my vision haunts
  When I to calm aspire :
Her phantom presence thrills and daunts :
I hear her base and mocking taunts
  Crackle from out the fire !

In vain with water and with tears
  Those flames I strive to quell ;
Each smoking ember at me leers,
And still that glowing face appears,
  And beckons me to hell !

BERGENHEIM.

On the sloping banks of the mystic Rhine,
   'Neath the grim old crumbling turret's gloom,
Where the lurid eyes of the gray owls shine,
   And the moon's gair rays the shades illume,

There I musing lay till a far church tolled
   Its long, sad, echoing midnight bell;
And I watched the ripples as they rolled
   On silvery pebbles ere they fell.

While I sat and gazed on the winding stream,
   As it ebbed and pulsed in fulvid sheen,
I ardently prayed for a power supreme
   To fathom those lucid depths unseen.

And I dreamt of a fatal day gone by.
   My poor heart grew sad, and dreary, too;
For that haunted Rhine heard my love's last sigh,
   When she perished in its waves so blue.

But the sombre glint of the moonbeams pale
   My sick soul thrilled to the very core,
As I sudden heard the last dying wail
   Of a voice I knew in days of yore!

The old, crumbling tower shone with weirdic glare,
   The night-owls screeched and the ravens croaked,
As that siren voice, in a feverish prayer,
   From the lustrèd waves my name invoked.

39

The fair form I saw on the waters float
  Of a spectral maiden, wondrous fair ;
The brown alga wove round her slender throat,
  And the golden sea-shells decked her hair.

'Twas the spirit sad of my love, my pride,
  That glided by in her cherub grace ;
And I sat on the lonely bank and cried,
  But in ev'ry tear I saw her face.

I can ne'er forget that sweet, melting gaze,
  Or that tender glance she cast on me,
As she sank below in the watery maze
  Of circling eddies to join the sea.

And where'er I linger, where'er I roam,
  Her spirit follows with languid eye,
And I see my love in her shroud of foam,
  And I hear her last wild gurgling sigh !

THE BALLAD OF GASTOUN.

THIS is a song of olden times,
    An odd, mediæval lay :
In jargons strange, and wondrous rhymes,
It still is sung by bards and mimes,
And oft is heard in distant climes,
    From Fez to fair Cathay.

In feudal ages stood a tower,
 In beauteous Normandy,
Where dwelt a lord, whose boundless power
Caused nigh six hundred slaves to cower,
While countless riches were his dower,
 And hosts of soldiery.

Yclept Gastoun, the Dauntless Knight,
 A man ignoring fear:
And tales of his chivalric might,
At tournament and open fight,—
At early morn or dead of night,—
 Are told since many a year.

Gallant was he with ladies fair,
 Clad in his coat of mail:
For bright blue eyes and russet hair
No other could with him compare,
Or, when in ire, he would prepare
 A parapet to scale.

On lute and rebec he could play
 Sad ditties to the moon:
While none could sing a ballad gay,
A churchly hymn, or roundelay,
And sweet words with more feeling say,
 Than handsome Knight Gastoun.

To him full many a noble dame
 Her love strove to impart:
No lily hand his hand could claim,
No eye could meet his eye of flame,
No ardent glance his breast could tame,—
 He broke, but took no heart.

At jousts and combats Gastoun shone
  'Midst flower of chivalry :
By damsels crimson scarfs were thrown,
And kisses sweet to him alone,
But failed to turn a heart of stone
  Spurning all rivalry.

He wore his 'scutcheon on his breast,
  With strange, antique device :
Helmets, torqued snakes, and fretted crest,
Proved that Gastoun had stood the test
Of struggles wild, with noble zest,
  For he was knighted thrice.

In his career of blood and strife,
  And battles with the foe,
His vassals wondered why a wife
Unto his breast, with trouble rife,
He did not take to cheer his life
  When older he should grow.

He spurned all ladies, free, high-born,
  And shunned their tempting eyes ;
The fairest maidens viewed with scorn,
Leaving them all to weep and mourn,
By passion's keenest anguish torn,—
  None owned him as a prize.

But once at hunt he met a maid,
  A peasant, plump and wee :
To her his knightly homage paid,
A sudden ardor there betrayed,
And brought her home in silks arrayed
  To beauteous Normandy.

The nuptial nights without delay
  Were fixed for Hallow Eve;
But, to the castle's sore dismay,
The king of France sent word that day,
Bidding his noble swift obey,
  Both bride and domains leave,

To follow o'er the sea his king,
  And join the great Crusade :
In honor of the Lord to sing,
The heads of Infidels to wring,
Saladin to submission bring,—
  Either by faith or blade.

So Gastoun called his men-at-arms
  And gorgeous retinue,
Bade adieu to his bride's fair charms,
Soothing her heart from vague alarms,
And swore to kill Turks by the swarms
  If she would remain true.

" And furthermore," the baron quoth,
  " Lambkin, I'll not be long :
And though to leave thee I am loth,
Remember that a sacred oath
Binds us forever troth to troth,
  Whether for right or wrong."

Then lept upon his prancing steed,
  And briskly rode away;
For France and for King Louis bleed,
E'er to sustain the holy creed,
The victory for Christ to speed,
  And at his tombstone pray.

And all the chivalry of France
   Embarked upon the seas,
To rouse the Moslems from their trance,
To gird the sword and wield the lance,
Handle the axe, and join, perchance,
   In joyous revelries.

For long long years in Palestine,
   In those brave days of eld,
The valiant knights in battle line,
With hearts of steel, though look benign,
With faith for friend, and cross for sign,
   The holy cause upheld.

He fought the Sultan Kelaoun,
   Upon an open plain
Of Syria's wastes, one sultry noon.
And here the turbaned Turk fell soon
Beneath the sharp glaive of Gastoun,
   Which clove his skull in twain.

And when the knight returned at last
   To sunny Normandy,
He spurred his charger on right fast,
By dust and traveling harassed,—
While his desire was unsurpassed
   His winsome bride to see.

But as he neared the fortress gate
   A herald tidings bore ;
To wit : that he returned too late
To see his fair and chosen mate,
Who, stricken down by cruel fate,
   Had died a year before.

At first the warrior ne'er replied,
    Though many saw him weep :
He strove not then his grief to hide,
But said, with all his Norman pride,
" I swore that she would be my bride ;
    That sacred oath will keep !

" Prepare for me the nuptial-room,
    My sturdy helots all :
Light up the turret's densest gloom,
Let tocsin ring, and culverin boom,
Then bring her coffin from the tomb
    In the ancestral hall !

" And let her bones in silk be clad :
    A crown placed on her head ;
And though my heart be sick, and sad,
My duty makes me feel more glad ;
And woe to him who saith I'm mad
    A skeleton to wed !"

The tower-bells chimed in mellow tones,
    The wedding hour was near :
While urchins young and wrinkled crones
Stood on tiptoe, with cries and groans,
To see the jagged and reeking bones,
    And witness scene so drear.

From out the crypt a long escort
    Of monks all clad in serge
A massive, iron-clasped coffin brought,
By crafty workmen richly wrought,
And laid it in the baron's court,
    Chanting a dismal dirge.

5

His strange commands were then obeyed
  By all the trembling throng,—
Though cowed by awe and sore afraid,
The skeleton in robes arrayed,—
While minstrels wedding anthems played,
  And all joined in the song.

And then this brave and loyal knight
  The shiny forehead kissed ;
And while the priest swooned from affright,
He swore to hold that nuptial rite
Sacred each day, sacred each night,
  All years he would exist.

" This vow," he cried, " I ne'er shall break ;
  Or if I so should do,
I hope to perish on the stake,
I hope that hell my soul shall take
And drown it in the fiery lake,
  If I should prove not true!"

Then sternly on his vassals frowned,
  And thrilled though undismayed :
Said, " Let my bride with gems be crowned,
Then firmly in a coffin bound,
And build a tombstone and a mound
  Where her dear bones are laid."

He spake, and from the palace door
  Rode gallantly away ;
Whether he left the Norman shore
For foreign lands we all ignore,
For he was never heard of more,
  And time will not betray.

VENICE.

O'ER Venice the proud
Night wraps its gray shroud ;
Dull torches illume
The arches and gloom.
The curled wavelets roll,
The convent bells toll
The hour of midnight,
While placid and bright,
O'er the dark lagoon,
Shines an opal moon.

The gondolas rest,
By tide-waves caressed.
From every side
In the churches glide
Fair women, who pray
For true love alway :
And tanned men who kneel,
For purses to steal,
While o'er the lagoon
Stares the opal moon.

With passion replete,
Yet tender and sweet,
Some soft serenade
Swells out from the shade.

47

A silvery voice
Will some maid rejoice,
Who whispers, "My love,
Climb quickly above,"
While o'er the lagoon
Smiles the opal moon.

But oft in the night
Sharp poignards gleam bright.
On the Bridge of Sighs
A dead body lies,
While the watchman's bell
Tolleth out "all's well."
And a victim's blood
Drips down in the mud,
While o'er the lagoon
Frowns the opal moon. . . .

Far out on the bay,
'Twixt green islets, play
The foam-ripples fair.
By the dazzling glare
Of the lantern's red light,
Young lovers take flight.
And past shadows dim,
Through cobalt waves skim,
While o'er the lagoon
Grins the opal moon.

Some funeral dirge
Blends low with the surge,
Which beats on the shore,
Deep-tonèd of roar.

Sad Venice so drear,
Sleeps ever in fear,
Whole ages have flown,
And no change is shown,
When o'er the lagoon
Beams an opal moon.

PHRYNE.

A MORE than regal Greek, proud Phryne stands,
Superb, majestic, most entrancing fair,
Smiling with insolent, contented joy—
Upon her matchless form of panting flesh.
While, draped in shadows of voluptuous gloom,
The tresses undulate of her long hair
Falling unkempt, in aureate silken sheen
Upon her bare mooned shoulders, white as fleece,
Her crescent bosom, and her pliant torse,
Would stir a fever in a heart of bronze,
For, pleased with budding youth and houri charms,
There lurks a glance electric in her orbs:
Gulfs, glowing with unutterable lust,
Languid, yet taunting, rich with ebon gleam ;
While vaulted, coral-nippled breasts of fire,
Wrapped in long gauzen robes of graceful fold,
Struggle in throbbing strength to burst their gyves,
And full unveil the glorious view of heat—
In vain subdued, forever seething o'er,
In all the angry unbaulked power of love.
Flooding her dimpled nac'rat siren cheek,

Rubied by blushes, she can ne'er conceal
Which spread through that imperious form divine,
Yearning to revel, carnally intense,
In fiercest throes of concupiscent bliss.
While Circe-spells spring from her melting gaze,
Resistless, mighty, arrogant, supreme!
Towering in passion's royal foaming coils,
Which must intolerable be to *feel*,
And prove a tempter to a faith-girt saint.
See, the pearl-studded chalice in her hand
She grasps, while o'er its scintillating brim
Flows the Falernian nectar, sweet and rich,
Exhaling mordant fumes of savory grape,
Luring soul-damning, riotous unrest
To fill a heart o'erladen with desire,
Invincible, erotic, scorning bounds:
While Greece, enamored at her jeweled feet,
Offers a nation's ransom for one beam
Of pungent ardor from her cloy-lit eyes,
Or yet to feel the candent contact choice
Of her round limbs, which madly would excite
And drown the soul of the most am'rous known
In wanton seas of bliss ineffable!

NON CREDO.

I, AS a lover, gloat
　　When gazing on some fond
　　Fair beauty frail and blonde,
And as I chat, to note
　　How my false words inspire
　　Her latent love desire.

A strange and mystic charm,
　　A magnetizing spell,
　　A secret none can tell,
Too subtle for alarm,
　　Pervades her witchèd sense
　　With mysteries immense.

I poison with a glance,
　　The venom of my look
　　No beauty's eye can brook,
Save in the languid trance,
　　Which, summoned by my power,
　　Causes a blissful hour.

I ask no favors yet,
　　The beauty offers all ;
　　Her roscid liplets call
Eager for kissing wet ;
　　And passion is the source
　　Whence flows my magic force.

Her face, with heat aflush,
　　Is kissed by am'rous air—
　　She breathes, while floods of hair
Hide not her bosom's blush ;
　　Her parchèd mouth is weak,
　　Powerless is tongue to speak.

Her hand is clasped in mine,
　　Her fulgid half-closed eyes,
　　Dimmed by a mute surprise,
No longer blink and shine ;
　　Ecstatic odors deep
　　Amort those eyes in sleep.

And still I cannot love
　　That beauty as she sighs :
　　I am her only prize ;—　　　.
Yet, as she looks above,
　　Mine orbs see not her youth,
　　My mind's eye sees the *truth*.

And then, her eyes so blue
　　Vanish before my stare ;
　　Stern truths my vision glare,—
Stern, bitter, saddest view ;
　　Two cavities of bone
　　I see, and that alone !

Her hot and pulsing breast
　　Withers before my sight ;
　　A picture of affright
Fills my mind doubt-oppressed ;
　　Her laughing mouthlet leers,
　　A skeleton appears !

Each beauty is the same,
　Hell gives me power to win;
　I force them to the sin,
And can resistance tame;
　Their sweet joy is my pain,
　I cannot love again.

In vain I strive to find
　The rapture I can give;
　My riot soul must live
In fancies dull and blind;
　Illusion, fraud, and guile
　Is woman's sweetest smile.

And at an age when men
　Love with their youth and might,
　I find but rot and blight
With my grim skeptic ken;
　No beauty can I trust,
　I see but bone and rust!

With satin and with silk
　They deck and clothe their frames;
　Their breath is hot as flames,
Their breast is white as milk,
　Yet they will always' be
　But skeletons for me.

SPLEEN.

ALL is sad ! all is sad !
When the soul's gangrene
   Belcheth out from the brain
   Its rank torrent, to stain
     A mind mad—
With the nausea of spleen.

All is gloom ! all is gloom !
When foul thoughts, knife-keen
   Venom life and its joys.
   When existence annoys,
     And the tomb
As a great Light is seen.

All is lost ! all is lost !
When our bliss terrene
   Fails to cure the dire plague
   Of gloom-thoughts sad and vague,
     Of life crossed
By the gall-kiss of spleen.

ARABESQUE.

An Orient sun with dazzling rays
    On Stamboul shone.
The mosques had closed, the muezzin's gong
    Had ceased to moan.
The golden minarets, clad in sheen,
    Glittered like fire.
A silence o'er the city fell,
    Sombre and dire.

The blue-waved Bosphorus alone
    Serene, at rest,
Ebbed idly round the gilded caïques
    Rocked on its breast.
While fishermen, on either shore,
    Basked in the sun,
Invoking Allah's grace in dreams
    Ill fates to shun.

The Sultan, Abdul Medjid Khan,
    Gazed on the sea,
From the court of "Silv'ry Crescent,"
    In revery ;
Inhaling clouds of pearly smoke
    From hookah tipped,
As he slowly and with relish
    His Mocha sipped.

55

Pastilles, perfumed of incense rare,
    Burned by his side.
Swart eunuchs watched his ev'ry sign
    Alert, lynx-eyed.
Refreshing sherbets, nedds, and wine
    Before him lay.
Quaint bearded dwarfs—fair odalisks—
    Stood to obey.

He murmured low the Sala sweet,
    Drooping his head,
And breathed a rice-bound papiros
    Latakia fed.
Then gazed out on the sunny court,
    Out on the " Horn,"
A gaze sad, long, and lingering,
    A gaze forlorn.

Weary of life was proud Abdul
    Of zebraed domes ;
Sickened of all the revelries
    Where th' Euxine foams.
His spires and tekkès, towers and mosques,
    Brought no content ;
And it seemed as if by sadness
    His soul was rent.

The harem long had ceased to charm,
    Though chosen slaves
Graced its poetic labyrinths,
    Sacred as graves.

His wrinkled vizirs still were true,
    And blessed his name,
While turbaned zaims and agas fought
    For Crescent's fame.

What was it then that deep annoyed
    The satrap's whims?
What fierce, relentless, gnawing spleen
    Unnerved his limbs?
Could he not consolation find
    In music's ties?
In melody's warm sympathies
    To banish sighs?

Love and affection soothed him not,
    Nor eased his mind;
Despite fame, pomp, and glory,
    Poor Abdul pined.
The Koran's holy precepts failed
    To cheer his brain,
And a cure for melancholy
    He sought in vain.

But sudden rose the Eastern prince,
    With visage staid,
Uttered an order to a slave,
    Who swift obeyed.
A chiseled box of scented wood
    Brought he, with fan;
The black attendants disappeared:
    'Lone stood the Khan.

With nimble hand turned he the lid,
　　Opened and gazed,
While in his nut-brown orbs a gleam
　　Of pleasure blazed.
Encased within, the sultan spied
　　A crimson paste,
Sweet-swelling, of sebaceous touch,
　　Of acrid taste.

The essence of an Arab plant,
　　Venom most dire,
Haschisch, in all its scarlet charm,
　　Glimmered like fire.
And yet the Sultan breathed its fumes
　　With joy supreme,
As hungry ghouls o'er clotted blood
　　Sniffle and scream.

With trembling grasp the prurient prince
　　In Mocha dipped
The contents of the fragrant box,
　　And savage, sipped—
The fiery drink that gnawed his heart,
　　Spurred on his brain,
Till utter chaos filled the soul,
　　And banished pain.

At first, a myth of beauty rare
　　Lulled him to rest.
He dreamt he stood in Paradise,
　　By Prophet blest.

In Eden's verdant groves he roamed,
    With glory crowned,
And, musing, thought that happiness
    He last had found.

But no ! the vision glided by,
    Houris, clad-white,
Gazed at him long and tenderly,
    Eyed-iolite.
In thrilling bliss he followed them
    Through fields of air ;
On, on, his febrile whim pursued,
    Befouled by care.

Crude angers boiled in Abdul's mind,
    By angels baulked.
With sullen voice and savage threat,
    In dreams he stalked.
The blue-eyed seraphim with smiles
    Tempted him near,
Then vanished in a flaky cloud,
    With jest and jeer.

Giant of stride, he paced the court
    With fiend-like laugh,
Pausing anon to seize his cup
    And poison quaff.
With madd'ning shriek and curdling oath
    Mahomet cursed,
Until his heart in agony,
    Gall-flushed, did burst.

With keen-edged scimitar he smote
    His slaves appalled.
And in his wild delirium,
    On Satan called !
The blood-red venom on his lips
    Foamed as he kecked ;
Rabid he bit, loon-frantic tore,
    Like demon checked !

Then, with a puma-bound, he sprang,
    With maniac yell,
To the open, sculptured casement,
    His road to hell !
Giddy and reckless, down he plunged,
    On spikes of stone,
And perished like an Infidel,
    Without a groan !

The sharp-toothed gateway pierced him through,
    And, as he hung,
The alarum-bell resounded,
    With brazen tongue.
His mangled corpse was taken down,
    In pomp arrayed,
While dervishes and imans knelt,
    And fervent prayed.

A vesper sun, with scarlet rays,
    On Stamboul shone ;
The mosques had closed, the muezzin's gong
    Had ceased to moan ;

The golden min'rets, clad in sheen,
    Glittered like fire ;
A silence o'er the city fell,
    Sombre and dire. . . . . .

SPIRIT VOICES.

WHAT can those spirit voices be,
Of such strange, solemn melody,
That are forever haunting me ?
    Sounds that I fear,
    Mystic and drear,
    Jarring my ear ;
Voices ever haunting me,
    What can they be ?

They come from the deep dark blue sea,
The restless, wavy, foam-tipped sea,
Weird voices ever haunting me ;
    When tempests roar,
    And billows pour
    Upon the shore,
I hear those voices haunting me,
    What can they be ?

When winds blow gently o'er the lea,
The rustling leaves of ev'ry tree
Are filled with voices haunting me ;
    6*

They sob and whine,
Through fir and pine,
And fragrant bine;
Those phantom voices haunting me,
What can they be?

They clang in kirk-bells' harmony,
They chant and laud, with fairy glee,
Those sombre voices haunting me;
With brazen peal
The echoes reel,
And o'er me steal;
Those spirit echoes haunting me,
What can they be?

Often I pray on bended knee
For strength the ghastly sound to flee,
Of voices ever haunting me;
With demon's skill,
Their laugh so shrill,
My senses thrill;
Those spectral voices haunting me,
What can they be?

And when I ask in agony
If e'er again I shall be free
From all those voices haunting me,
Fierce shadows loom,
And from the gloom
Point to a tomb,
Dug by the spirits haunting me!—
What can they be?

CANZONE.

I LOVE a cobalt sky,
    When the eye—
Dazed by the lucent view,
Errs in a world of blue—
Charmed by the sapphirine—
    Of its sheen.

Small sable clouds soar past,
    Airy fast :
Ere the storm has begun—
The calid golden sun,
Pierces them with its light,
    In their flight.

My heart is like the sky
    I descry ;
One vast expanse of joy—
With Love and Hope as buoy,
Ignoring days of woe—
    Here below.

Dark clouds of grief and pain,
    Pass in vain :
My mind is like the sun,
The clouds melt one by one—
In glorious streams of song,
    Light and long.

SONG OF UKRAINE.

WITH bleeding bit and frantic neigh,
   A horse nigh goaded unto pain,
Drags o'er the Dnieper's steppes a sleigh,
While, as he speeds, the ebbing day
   Darts its pale shadows on the plain.

The cutting blast in fury, stirs—
   Through veils of blinding snow and sleet
The raw, bleak, tempest-beaten firs,
As like a yielding arrow, whirrs—
   The panting beast, shod lightning fleet.

Within, a fur-wrapped female form,
   With virile nerve, the courser guides:
She heedeth not the whining storm,
Why should she care, her heart is warm—
   On! on! the light Kabitka glides.

Snug on her lap her infant lies
   Sheltered and safe from rime and frost:
The mother's gaze invokes the skies,
Tears, frozen stiff, bedim her eyes,
   Twelve dreary versts must still be crossed.

The tempest's wrath she does not fear,
   She cowers not 'neath the sheets of hail;
The houseless road is long and drear,
But buoyant hope is there to cheer—
   Its voice is stronger than the gale.

But hark ! what are those sounds that thrill
   The very marrow in her bones !
Raucous and horrid echoes chill
Her bubbling blood ; while sharp and shrill
   They mingle with the wind's sad moan.

Gaunt, hairy wolves, behungered, dash
   With frosty snort beside the sleigh :
She sees their small white teeth that gnash,
She sees their small fire-eyes that flash,
   She hears them clamor for their prey !

She shrinks :. their grisly jaws athirst,
   Close by her arm protrude and gape—
With vigorous blow she slays the first,
The others stop to feast—a verst
   Is gained ; and she may yet escape.

But no ! the shaggy brutes appear
   Bolder : hot blood has made them wild.
Pressed by the frenzy of their leer,
The swooning mother, mazed by fear,
   With vital shriek, hurls out her child !

  *   *   *   *   *   *   *   *

The glimmering of the day shines bright,
   Two horsemen to the village go :
They pause mid-road, and there alight,
For human bones, picked clean and white,
   Lay scattered o'er the thawing snow.

SOULS OF FIRE.

GLORY to thee, oh Soul of Fire!
The pulseless souls of gods expire,
But thou burn'st deathless in thine ire.
    Glory to thee!
Fattened on ruin, blight, and gore,
Soul lacking sense, for evermore
In spheres of wonder doomed to soar.
    Glory to thee!

Vassal of Satan, proudly stern:
Pity-castrated, made to spurn—
Anguish unheeding, blaze and burn!
    Glory to thee!
Once hadst thou altar, slave, and shrine,
Once hadst thou priest thy flame to tine,
Once as the powers of God didst shine.
    Glory to thee!

Now is thy sacred might austere,
By nescient mortals cursed in fear,
They cringe beneath thy crackling clear.
    Glory to thee!
But when their tortured bodies wring—
With scorching yaup; toucht by thy sting,
Recall thee that thy laws I sing.
    Glory to thee!

I dreamt, unnerved by feverish sleep,
That in an Aztec temple—deep—
Below its crypts, where mages keep
    The holy rites,
I wandered ; and with tremor viewed
The sacrifices fell, and rude,
Offered to queme the Fire Soul's mood
    And stay its spites.

The sacred flamelets lush and gair,
With vacillating bluish glare,
Blazed on a shrine of sculpture rare ;
    Guarded by priests :
While in the solemn site there strolled,
Two haughty lions, gaunt and bold,
Gloaring with fulvid eyes of gold
    For fleshy feasts !

Around the massive altars, soiled,
With clotted blood, with mire bemoiled,
Huge famished reptiles crept and coiled
    With slimy gyre.
While sizy tongue, erect and spiss,
With frenzied gape and jarring hiss,
Spat from foul fangs their venomed kiss
    Upon the fire !

Near to the hallowed spot lay bound,
With gyves and shackles, to the ground,
Victims fear-palsied by the sound
    Of snakes accursed.
Sentenced to glut their greedings dern
And Quetzalcoatl's anger turn :
For skin must char, and blood must burn,
    To slake his thirst !

Despite despairing wail and groan,
The martyrs in the vault are thrown,
Where to the Fire God's heart of stone
    They shriek for grace !
I see the serpents glide in swarms—
Their grumous clasp the cold limbs warms—
They wind about their quaking forms
    With tight embrace !

The lions shake their shaggy mane,
Their jaws are tinged with crimson stain,
Lust-howls blend low with howls of pain
    And gasps of dread !
The snakes with torpor fall inert,
The beasts o'ergorgèd wawl in dirt,
The Soul of Fire alone alert—
    Burns ruddy red ! . . . . .
        .

———————

Glory to thee ! oh Soul of Fire !
The pulseless souls of gods expire,
But thou burn'st deathless in thine ire.
    Glory to thee !

THE GHOUL.

Deep in the ombrèd labyrinth—
    Of a weird mystic wood,
Lost in a verdant maze of leaves,
    Four giant oak-trees stood.
And on their heavy nodous boughs,
    Strange speckled night-birds purled,
While round their knarry rugged trunks—
    The ivy lithely querled.

A gloomy, sombre silence reigned—
    In that sepulchral nook ;
Save when the doleful brumal blast,
    The crooked branches shook.
And then the wind-bent leaflets moaned—
    With low, uneasy sigh ;
Like the voice of wandering spirits,
    Lamenting through the sky.

Close by the ancient mammoth trees,
    Half hidden by the gloom—
Of curvèd firs, and stately pines,
    There stood a simple tomb,
Of rugose stone, besprent with moss,
    Of cryptish glaucous green,
That glistened like an emerald,
    Beneath the glow-worm's sheen.

The nearest hamlet kirk had tolled,
  The solemn, midnight hour.
And through the queach, its droning clang—
  Aroused an occult power.
For as the echo fainter grew,
  Upon the sulph'rous air;
A crescent moonbeam pierced the copse—
  And shone with phantom glare.

Then the huge oak-trees seemed to breathe!
  Their feathered inmates trilled!
While odd, mysterious footsteps near—
  The soul with panic filled!
A choking nidorous miasm foul—
  Spread through the haunted glade,
As slimy newts, and olid efts,
  Crept slowly from the shade!

A huntsman, lost within the wood—
  During the noonday's heat:
Had slept beneath the sturdy oaks,
  And, with kind rest replete
Now stretched his saggy, yielding limbs—
  And stirred his sluggish gaze;
To find the homeward path again,
  And leave the dreary maze.

But as he sought the welcome route—
  His wandering steps to guide:
He saw a wan, and pallid form,
  Forth from the thicket glide.

A maiden, clad in flowing robes—
    Of pure, and spotless white!
Who paused, and gazed with ravishment—
    Upon the tranquil site.

Ne'er had the hunter seen before,
    Such calm resplendent grace:
Ne'er had he dreamt in troubled sleep,
    Of such a gentle face!
Eyes soundless in vague depths of blue—
    Tresses of fulgid gold,
Lips like the carmine's ruddy glow—
    Form of a vieless mould!

Who can this sylph-like creature be
    Pensive before that stone?
Is she a myth, a fancied form—
    What seeketh she alone?
Sure 'tis some sorrowed maiden, come—
    O'er a loved grave to weep:
Why does she bend so eagerly?
    Why that death vigil keep?

Yet now she digs in frantic haste—
    The moist and turbid soil;
See how her soft and tender hands
    Seem heedless of the toil!
What has she found, she huggeth so?
    Strange! 'tis a form she holds—
So tightly, with such ouphic glee,
    And with her arms enfolds!

Heavens! she kisses it, and now—
    Her hands are red with *blood :*
While drops of clotted gore ooze fast,
    And trickle in the mud !
Hah! hah! that laugh, that sick'ning grin—
    She holds a putrid corpse !
See with what rage she biteth it !
    Look how she tears, and warps !

That spectral maiden, saintly meek—
    Was but a fiendish Ghoul :
Who carrion gorged, while hell-kites croaked
    Awed to obey her rule.
She bade them share her midnight feast
    And dabble in the gore,
And as they helped her cleave the flesh
    Then would she laugh the more !

The horror-stricken huntsman knelt—
    Breathing a fervent prayer :
Which blended with the grumbling low,
    Of cougars in their lair.
While elves, and gnomes, with flamant eyes
    Darted around the trees—
Adding their hootings to the owls,
    That mingled with the breeze.

This odious spot he fain would leave—
    And rose to steal away :
Only the siren Ghoul had *seen,*
    And scented other prey.

Seductive was her bell-like voice,
　　Magnetic was her will,
Alluring was her lascive glance—
　　Resistless was her skill !

She drew him near—and nearer still—
　　And clasped him in her arms :
Though all his angry soul rebelled,
　　From her blood-smearèd charms.
She nustled him with childish joy,
　　Upon her globous breast :
And with her reeking, gory lips—
　　His quivering form caressed !

Gyved by an unknown, subtle power,
　　Inert the hunter stayed :
While in a passion-blinded dream—
　　Her lustful will obeyed.
For with erotic fury fierce,
　　This Ghoulish scene of love
Passed 'neath the oak-tree's shade below,
　　The moon's wild leer above !

The demon drained her victim's fire,
　　Then vanished into space :
While all the stunted roytish gnomes,
　　Followed her burning trace.
But swift returned, to romp and dance,
　　With wild and raucous shout ;
Around the vimless, dying man—
　　His agony to flout.

A hazy mist, before the dawn—
    Was struggling with the sun :
Th' enchanted oak-trees, rustled low,
    Seeming its rays to shun.
But when its candent gleam had pierced
    The foliage and the gloom,
Two half-picked skeletons were seen,
    Clasped to the rugged tomb !

RÊVERIE.

OFTEN have I sat in wonder,
When the distant booming thunder,
Seemed to rend the sky asunder—
    With its hoarse discordant blare.
With its echoes loud resounding,
With its dull and heavy pounding,
Its alarum shrill rebounding,
    Through the cloudy ashy air.
While the forkèd lightning blazing,
The blue vault of Heaven upraising,
And the eye with terror dazing—
    With its lurid fulvid stare :
    With its livid ghastly glare :
    With its vivid flash and flare :
And its horrifying dazzle, of danger, and despair.

Long years ago I saw this sight :
One stormy boisterous winter's night,
Beneath a cresset's murky light,
    On the ocean deep and vast.

And I listened to the grumbling,
To the low and dismal rumbling,
And the incoherent mumbling,
    Of the keen and icy blast.
Stirring up a wild commotion,
On the surface of the ocean,
Filling me with strange emotion—
    While vague mem'ries of the past:
    In my mind's eye gathered fast:
    Each one sadder than the last:
Fantastic, dreamy glimpses, of the unforgotten Past.

As I mused on that and this,
Harked I to the tempest's hiss,
Heard I its cold chilly kiss ;
    On the desert cliffs of stone.
While above the clouds soared scowling,
And the frigid blasts kept howling,
With a rigid mystic growling,
    And with wild and savage groan.
My sad rhapsodies all shocking,—
The mad waves eternal rocking,—
Seemed my anguish to be mocking,—
    As I sat there all alone:
    Listening to their monotone:
    And their whining sigh and moan:
Warning me, then and forever, for all sinnings to atone.

And their brusque incessant splashing,
In dense sheets of surf-sheen dashing,
The gaunt cliffs and beaches lashing,
    With their everlasting pour.

My poor heart with tremor filling,
All my numbèd senses thrilling,
And my very marrow chilling,
    With their dull and sullen roar.
As the billows onward creeping,
O'er each other playing, leaping,
Time by smaller wavelets keeping,
    On the surf-bespangled shore :
    As they did in days of yore :
    As they will for evermore :
With their never-ceasing clamor, and their rough and
    raucous roar.

I saw ships all cleft and shattered,
With their rigging torn and tattered,
With their decks and bulwarks battered,
    By the fierce and bitter gale.
The billows wild and wilder grew—
As o'er their crests, the doomed ships flew,
To soundings, where the tempest knew,
    They would find no helping sail.
Where engulfed by ocean's panic,
And the sea-god's rage satanic,
'Neath the lightning gleams volcanic,
    No survivor could unveil :
    The sad secret of the tale :
    Causing listeners to quail :
For ev'ry wretch aboard them, perished in the frantic
    gale.

With sad and sempiternal dirge,
Those fuming billows capped with surge,
Still revel on the ocean's gurge,
    By the shrieking breezes fanned.

Like a mighty limbèd giant,
Stalwart sinewy defiant,
Tortuous flexile deep and pliant,
    Still roll on in splendor grand.
Ever ebbing, pulsing, beating,
In round bubbling eddies meeting,
Their odd vagaries repeating,
    Playing on the pebbled sand :
    On the lone and dreary strand :
    With a power none can withstand :
Sent there by some grand eternal, strange and solemn
    unknown hand.

I still sit on that barren shore ;
And listen to the angry roar—
Of care and sorrow as they pour,
    In the Ocean of my mind.
My ships of Hope, are wrecked and lost,
My whims and wishes spurned and crossed,
By sternest Fate with heart of frost,
    Cheerless, pitiless, unkind.
And so 'tis ever throughout life,
Nothing but turmoil, woe and strife,
A painful dream with tempests rife,
    Baffling us like helpless blind.
    If for calm we once have pined :
    Surely comes some frigid wind :
To chill our hopes, until in Death, we can a balsam
    find.

SONNET.

I of a fiend the heart had, thou as God
Good and most lenient, merciful soul-kind,
Forgave my mutiny and rebel mind
Aye! when thy hand could wield the avenging rod
When at thy will thou couldst have crushed to sod,
(Barren and foul of thought like mine, where blind
I culled the dirt I threw thee, hadst thou pined
To hurl thy sdains upon my cringing nod
That all avowed!) yet thou wert nobly good,
As 'neath thy scathing gaze abashed I stood,
Penitent, pallid by fierce shames, but thou
Pardoned me all—my heinous sin and more;
Does not the yielding wood of santal bough
Perfume the cruel axe that strikes its core?

SONNET.

From out the deep dark glooms of doubt and pain,
    Thy love's star-radiance, nascent, soon shall shine.
Splendent of carnal glamour from thy brain
    Like precious stones behued in tints divine,
That hide in dazzling depths a soul long lain,
    A spirit crystallized, infused, benign!

The gem ignores its soul's deep glowing vein,
    Thy soul ignores the gem-love that is thine !
But I have come to fray the path to spheres
    Whose secret thrills, whose dizzy height endears,
For I will revel in their glorious gloom,
    Born to enjoy the wonders of thine eyes—
The riot splendors of their vague perfume,
    Thy soft and amorous symphonies of sighs—— !

PARIS.

Thou noblest and fairest of cities—
    Art scoffed at by others for Sin ;
They lavish their taunts, and mock pities,
    On the vices thou brewest within :
    They gloat o'er thy ruin ; and grin—
When they sing of thy name in their ditties.

They belch forth their vomit of slander,
    And their volleys of insults rain :
They tell thee 'twixt harlot and pander,
    That thy fame has rotted with stain :
    That thou strivest to rise in vain—
Aye ! they tell thee all this in their candor

Unarmed, when thou fell'st in war's chasms
    Did they e'er lend a pitying ear ?
In the throes of death, did thy spasms
    Dim their eyes with a single tear ?
    No : but cynical smile they and leer
When they tell thee thy hopes are but phasms !

Yet they loved thee when rich and merry,
   Thy streets ran with gold and with wine !
How to cloy of thy sweets was their query—
   They praised thee as peerless, divine,
   And thou thought'st not when bowed at thy shrine,
That their gall in thy wounds they would bury.

With the gloss of their speech have they oiled thee,
   Till reckless thou satedst their thirst :
With the mud of their lusts have they soiled thee
   With the stench of their breath accursed :
   Till thine heart of proud hearts did burst—
When of name and of fame they despoiled thee.

Thy beauty deflowered, they abase thee,
   They ravished thy virtue of yore :
The hounds now yearn to disgrace thee,
   They sweated to make thee a whore—
   But they sigh for thy charms as before—
And clamor like beasts to embrace thee !

Be it so : they a bawd have begotten—
   And thy shrine is bespattered with grime ;
But for thinkers thy sins are forgotten,
   For thou blushest not in thy crime,
   While thy cavillers hide in slime—
The foul secrets of vices more rotten !

PARIS, August, 1872.

À . . . .

CELLE que j'ai le plus aimée
Avait la taille d'une almée,
   De gros yeux bleus au long cil noir.
Un teint de rose et de neige,
Comme l'Albâne et le Corrège
   Seuls dans le rêve ont pu voir.

Ses cheveux plus bruns que l'ébène
Trainaient comme un manteau de reine
   Sur un corps aux divins contours.
Sa bouche était petite et rose,
On eût dit deux feuilles de rose—
   Où nichait un essaim d'amours.

Ses deux mains tenaient dans la mienne
Dans le baiser sa fraiche haleine
   Avait des effluves de feu.
Sa voix était un doux poème,
Et quand elle me disait "je t'aime"
   Je me sentais devenir Dieu—!

.

THE SIREN.

'NEATH long lashes,
  Sea-spray wet :
Gleams and flashes,
  Eye of jet—
Glancing dreamy,
  On a breast ;
White and creamy—
  Wave-caressed :
Tresses flowing
  Ambry light,
Liplets glowing
  Scarlet bright ;
Form of peri—
  Face of fay—
Arch and merry,
  Fair as day.
Jewel-laden,
  Zephyr-fanned,
Sits a maiden—
  On a strand,
Green and golden,
  In the sea—
Quaintly moulden,
  Like a Z.

———

Rubies precious,
　Ocean pearls
Light the meshes—
　Of her curls.
Towards the islet,
　In a boat—
Steers a pilot,
　Come to gloat—
On the creature,
　Siren-charmed—
On each feature,
　Unalarmed :
Near, and nearer,
　Glides the bark—
Clear, and clearer,
　Shines the spark—
Of her glancing,
　While her smile—
Soul entrancing,
　Masks its guile :
Lures him ravished
　To her feet,
Bliss unlavished
　Long and sweet—
For his sorrows
　Full atones ;
On the morrow
　Naught but bones—
Rot, half eaten,
　Mixed with sand :
Billow-beaten,
　On that strand,

> Green and golden,
> In the sea—
> Quaintly moulden,
> Like a Z.

PICTURETTE.

There's a gloom on the Bridge of Sighs,
  A gloom on the dark lagoon :
The ripples swell—the ripples rise
As over its deep, cold water, plies—
  The glare of the silv'ry moon.

There's a light on the Bridge of Sighs—
  The light of a lantern's flame :
A mantled form in ambush lies—
Grim ashy clouds course o'er the skies,
  The moon hides its face in shame.

There's a step on the Bridge of Sighs,
  The step of a cavalier
Some maiden trysts, and swift he hies
To kiss and fondle a lovely prize,
  As he speeds, the moon shines clear.

There's a sound on the Bridge of Sighs,
  The sound of a struggle loud,
A dagger gleams: a shadow flies,
An inert form on the pavement lies,
  The moon goes behind a cloud. . . . .

FANTAISIE.

DRAPED in light robes, with tarbouked noul,
  I love, half dreaming, to admire—
My chibouque's round and polished bowl,
  And watch the glow of opium's fire.
Nacarat, golden, from my soul—
  Its sensuous crackling can inspire—
Rare fancies, which my mind console,
  When fading in each smoky gyre.

An Indian temple, massive, grand,
  Looms 'fore my sight, and towers in air—
Erected by a sorcerer's hand,
  Of architecture strangely rare.
While near its sculptured portals stand—
  Cohorts of slaves, and almées fair,
Dancing their quaint-tuned saraband,
  With bronze-tanned skin, and floating hair.

I rove within the Shiraz vale,
  Where onyx fountains jut and play,
Where budding roses, pink and frail,
  Bend rorid 'neath their floods of spray:
I slumber midst the lilies pale—
  I listen to the linnet's lay,
The subtle powers I quaff, unveil—
  Sweet dreams of everlasting day.

Far in a mosque I can discern,
   Vischnou's and Siva's altars high ;
I see the sacred fires that burn—
   With quivering flamelets to the sky.
I see the dolmaned Guebers stern,
   Worship their igneous god, and try—
With contrite hearts to win and earn,
   The honor by his hand to die.

I soar in dreams, and ravished hear,
   Sung by some bard of Gulistan ;
A moallak soothing to the ear,
   An echo of the caravan—
Which passes by, morose and drear,
   Out from the town ; while, mute, I scan
The kandjared guards, with uncouth gear,
   Pacing the streets of Ispahan.

On fair Corea's shellèd stream,
   My fancy floats without restraint ;
Pagodas, wrought in porcelain, teem—
   On every side, of fabric quaint.
While genii pleased my sense to queme,
   The blue-foamed Yang-ste-Kiang, faint—
Before my gaze depict in dream,
   Ebbing its ripples with my plaint.

Traversing spheres, I undismayed,
   Revel my view in Stamboul's sheen ;
Mahomet's chosen, pomp arrayed—
   Laden with glittering damascene--

Passes with haughty cavalcade,
  Armed to the teeth with scimitars keen,
While o'er the turrets of Belgrade—
  I see the argent min'rets gleen !

In Norway's fields, each frozen fjiord,
  Recalls the old chivalric time :
The noble Saga of the Sword,
  The Eddas told in Runic rhyme.
Olaf and Frithiof, with their horde—
  Of stalwart warriórs, chapped by rime,
For me still battle on that sward,
  And chant their anthems in Drontheim.

Upsala's rugose steeples dart—
  Their granite splendor through the air ;
Odd marvel of old Northern art,
  Is this sad, solemn site of prayer.
And 'fore the shrines, so chill and swart—
  Kneel suff'ring sinners, bent by care,
As on the rough-hewn steps, the mart—
  Begins its bustle, and its blare.

The opium's Spirit, ah my quest,
  Changes the scene to fair Sèville :
Where alamedas, sun-love blessed,
  The atmosphere with perfumes fill,
While jet-eyed damsels err or rest
  Beneath the shade of trellised vill—
Taunting their gallants to a test,
  And time with cigarillos kill.

Along the Chiaja, as I stroll—
  Vesuvius belches forth its fire:
But I can free, untrammeled troul—
  Deep in its jaws, and brave its ire.
With wingèd feet from pole to pole,
  The spirits lead, and never tire.
The depth of depths is then my goal,
  The inner world is mine entire!

Th' embattled turrets of the Rhine,
  Sombre and breme, now greet my sight:
O'erhead the lucent asters shine,
  Shedding their calm opaline light.
I see within, elate with wine,
  The earnest face of dame and knight,
Quaffing the nectar of the vine—
  Narrating tales of love and fight.

Without, I see the mystic dells,
  The frisky, fire-haired gnomes at play:
I hear the dorf-kirk's mellow bells—
  I hear the wand'ring minstrel's lay.
The Elfen-King his host expels,
  To gambol till the dawn of day—
While ouphs and fairies brew their spells,
  And toothless witches seek their prey.

On Egypt's arid wastes, the Sphinx—
  Startles my mind, now opium-drunk:
My chain of thought, ungyved by links,
  Deep on the dreggy Nile is sunk.

I hear the snorting of the lynx,
    The egret's shriek, the crane's dull crunk,
The mammoth eye of Memnon winks—
    Chilling my ken, smoke-worn and shrunk.

I see huge Cheops' tortuous crypt,
    Its labyrinths so chilly dark :
I see its antique vaults time-nipped,
    Its shrivelled mummies stiff and stark—
The ibex and the sacred script,
    The Copt's odd hierarchic mark,
The iron urnlets jewel-tipped—
    And cinerous wealth of dust and chark.

Fleeing cloud-wrapped, refreshed, I pass—
    From out the sod of colcothar :
To view the giant Kremlin's mass—
    Novgorod's domes, and Kazan's star.
Here hirsute moujiks rough and crass,
    Swear by their saints, and by their Czar—
O'er ev'ry mug of creamy Kvas,
    They tipple with their Kaviar.

My balmful drug lends power to sate—
    The novel yearns for which I ache :
Its genii as I meditate—
    My thirst for airy whims can slake.
And with their skill, by gods innate,
    O'er worlds and spheres my spirit take,
Until my sleep-cloyed eyes nictate,
    And I from my mad wandering wake

LINES TO AN OPAL.

Thou fire-veined stone of mystic hue!
Tell me, if by thy spell-gaze true—
   Thou canst my thoughts reveal?
And in thy depths of lucid sheen,
Imprisoned by thy sapphirine,
Is there a hidden soul unseén—
   Watching with fairy zeal?

What lurks within thy mottled heart?
Why do lush henna-crimsons dart—
   Through thy vexed, lustrous eye?
Then ebb, and flow, from Kalan dyed,
Into an orient sunny tide,—
Of glaucous gloss, thy gemmèd pride,
   Only to fade and die.

Is it the spirit weird, and wild,
Of some strange, spectral ouphen child—
   By stunted Kobolds spurned?
Who slyly dwelleth in thy breast,
Showing its grateful impish zest,
By varied hue whene'er caressed—
   Or towards a sunbeam turned.

Set in thy bezil of wrought gold,
Shimmering in thy matchless mould—
   Thou clingest to my hand.

And, when the warm flesh burns and glows
Thy ruby tinge, lascivious, shows—
The ardor that resistless grows,
   From touchy nerve to gland.

Oh! how I gloat to see the flush,
Precursor of thy am'rous blush—
   Whene'er of Love I sing!
Oh! how thy wavy sphere of fire—
Pulses, and quobs, of mad desire—
When 'neath hot kisses I admire,
   Thy iridescent ring!

From a rich-tinted emerald blaze,
Thou grin'st at me, with hate, to craze —
   And tempt my latent ire!
Then in a crystal topaz glance—
Thy spirit calls a dreamy trance,
My own wild tremor to enhance,
   Like Quetzalcotlian fire!

And when by gloomy pain and cark—
I pine: then deadened in thy spark,
   Vanished thy fulgor bright!
For like a glassy troutlet's eye—
Filmy and hueless dost thou lie,
Thy nacker dimmed, like spotted sky—
   Awaiting ebon night.

Thou tell'st me if my love is true,
For in thy azure smile so blue,
   Sunlight and glory shine.

The buoyant hope of thy mild glare,
Dispels the myriad-wingèd care ;
And thy fond pressure seems to share,
   Joys that are ever mine.

The purple ray thou oft hast worn,
Cometh alone when soul is torn—
   By pangful, chafing grief.
Then in its lilac flood I see,
Thy tearful eye gaze up at me,
Condoling with my agony—
   Cheering beyond belief.

But, when my love is guileful found,
Then is thy face with saffron crowned,
   Effulgent and severe !
Thou goad'st me on by wily skill—
Thy fiendish orders to fulfil—
And shunning pity speed, and kill—
   The fair one I love dear.

Magnetic is thy wondrous power ;
And 'neath its gnomish strength I cower,
   Gyved in its awful spell.
For by thy sdainful, ochreous leer—
Inspired—I will not quake or fear,
If legions of thy damned appear—
   To drag me to their Hell !

Aye ! for thy mad ignescent light,
Bewitching soul of crafty sprite ;
   Serves me as friend and foe.

Thy magic ogling tells me all—
While here on Earth—but if I fall—
Then will thy lurid gleam appal,
   A sinful soul below.

TO . . . . .

WHY wouldst thou thoughtless spurn the easing sweet
   I offer to thy spleen-toucht, waiting life—
Of patient yearn, of baffled, heart-hushed strife?
   Are not thy crying love-lusts sharp as knife?
Dreamy as music; hot as lava heat?
   Why, when I beg thee at thy tiny feet
Dost thou refuse? when body—bosom—rife,
   Thy am'rous answerings my bold queries meet.

If thy heart's fancy willeth, why delay?
   For will it doth; with youth's and craving's might
Those riot joys, acme of world's delight
   Rest with thy simple soul's yea—so, ignite
Crude, mordant flames of ardor, that can stay,
   And check all sweeter blisses by their sway
Until dreams olden can a new dream cite,
   Till whims blood-satisfied can fade away.

AFFINITIES.

A VIEWLESS phantom of sweet sound
   Lingers within my ravished brain ;
Scarce have I all its dream-notes found—
Its thread of melody unwound—
   When strange ! I lose the magic strain.

I muse, while ev'ry fibre rings,
   And list again with avid ear
To charm the harmony it sings—
And tempt upon its tuneful wings—
   That echo of a godlier sphere.

But ah ! I cannot break the spell
   Although it haunteth me the same :
But I have learnt to know it well—
And think its meaning I can tell—
   For 'tis my heart that sighs thy name.

DIMINUENDO.

DOWN by the desert beach I wander.
Lone on the frowning rocks I ponder.
Ired by the night-winds is my sorrow.
Dead is my soul to griefs of morrow.

The surging billows swell and rise,
The ashy color of the skies—
Blends with the chilly foam and spray,
Lit by the glare of fading day.
  The ebon clouds of night—
  Grin sternly in their flight ;
  The sombre waves in ire
  Are tinged with shadows dire.
   The breakers call me !
    Their voices are hoarse—
  Their forms appal me !
    They howl for my corse.
    The night is dark—
      The winds moan shrill,
    The cresset's spark,
     Illumes the hill.
      The storm's sigh—
      Rends the sky:
      And each wave,
      Seems a grave :
      On the shore—
      Billows pour,
      Waters weep—
      Mortals sleep :
      What is life ;
      But a strife ?
      May my end—
      Make amend.
      Night falls.
      Death calls.
      Night thrills.
      Death chills !

BRIDE AND DOG.

I LOVE my dog, I love my bride,
    The love is not the same—
    A taunting world may blame—
But all my joy, and all my pride,
Rest with the dog, when by my side
    He crouches, mute and tame.

My faithful hound will ne'er betray,
    He boundeth at my nod;
    I am his sire, his God!
Licking my feet, content to stay,
He asks no favors, care, nor pay,
    And loves me 'neath the rod.

Ready my life-blood to defend,
    His love is firm and long—
    In spite of kick or thong,
His only fear is to offend:
And then with grace to seek amend
    If I am right, or wrong.

My bride can love, but, can betray,
    The day when not caressed—
    A caprice fills her breast:
I never doubted, yet I say—
Let woman's love be as it may,
    I love my dog the best.

Oh sapless, silly laws of man!
   I cannot kill my bride—
   E'en should she have defied—
The churches' law, or holiest ban ;
For pity leers with visage wan—
   And bids my arm abide.

But for my dog, my noble pet
   At any time, my will—
   Gives me the right to kill :
Should I by anger, past forget—
And strike him down without regret
   Simply when feeling ill.

Alas ! this social power is used
   With heedless haste unjust :
   The dog and friend you trust,
Often is slain, though not accused—
Whereas the bride who faith abused,
   Lives to the world's disgust !

TURQUERIE.

THE waves of the Bosphorus dashed—
On Scutari, and splashed—
In the pale lunet's light.
Like a torrent of pearls,
While their glistening whirls,
Foamy bright—
Flashed.

The night was pacific and still,
Not a sound save the trill—
Of the bulbul was heard :
And a wind of perfumes,
From the horizon's glooms,
Gently stirred,
Chill.

Seráskier's turret, the Mosque,
Yeni Djami, its Kiosque,
And the dome of Selim—
Towered their portals and grees
Far above the yew-trees
Twilight dim,
Of bosk.

The Seraglio's beauty Asmé,
As the day ebbed away
With a wistful look, sad,

From her balcony gazed—
Where the sea-ripples blazed
   Star-lit mad
    Of ray.

Then arose from the glooms below
  A melody sweet, slow,
    The moon shone in the face—
  Of a young giaour fair,
  With curls of auburn hair,
    Rich of grace
     And glow.

The tone of his voice did entreat,
  His song swelled through the street
    Up to the skies above.
  Fond words of hope and pride—
  Fond words that fear defied—
    Songs of love
     Sweet.

But a struggle is heard—a head
  Is bathed in hot drops, red,
    A horrid crimson flood !
  The giaour sang to die
  Who now for him will sigh
    There in mud
     Dead !

The night is pacific and still,
  Not a sound save the trill
    Of the bulbul is heard ;
  And a wind of perfumes,
  From the horizon's glooms,
    Is stirred,
     Chill.

SANS CŒUR.

Of life I have tasted the sweet.
     Ay ! till my soul was sick :
Its bone, and its marrow, and meat,
     Did I pick—
The pith found I rot, and effete—
     To lick !

Its pleasures are sapless of gust
     Rank and bitter as gall :
Brewing hatred, sin, mistrust,
     One and all—
While my heart's curse on them I thrust
     Like scall !

A joyful hour has been my quest,
     A simple quest sincere :
That hour of joy my soul caressed—
     I thought near :
The bliss *I* found was foul as pest
     And fear !

In unbelief my mind is cast,
     In Atheism wrought :
Though worlds of lore, and science vast,
     And of thought—
Have through my aching temples passed,
     Sin-fraught.

Of Love the flower I now ignore—
    Lost in a phantom world ;
Its yielding leaves in days of yore
    I unfurled :
A *worm* in every deep rich core—
    Had curled !

Honors attract me not, and gold—
    No more than common lead,
Can by its temptings manifold,
    Turn my head :
And warm a heart twice polar-cold
    And dead !

With breath of myrrh, and touch of fire,
    Kindled by demons base :
Passions alone and lusts, inspire—
    My wan face :
And softly turn my rankling ire
    To grace.

All is illusion, fraud and sin,
    Tear, anguish, trust, or smile—
Falsehood without—falsehood within—
    World of guile—
Devils pray now, and angels grin—
    With bile !

From power of love, to power of purse,
    From childhood's fondest ties :
And from the cradle to the hearse,
    Or from the skies—
Nothing in life is worth a curse,
    All lies !

No heart have I, no faith, no hope,
  Sorrow, nor pain, nor care :
Willing to die by axe or rope
  Here, or there—
Defying Heaven's horoscope
  And prayer.

Ambition learnt I to forget
  As would a dog a bone :
Remorse my heart in vain can fret,
  'Tis of stone :
Mine eyes by tears are never wet
  When 'lone—

Gods do I spurn, creeds have I none,
  Religions I deride :
Believe in naught—and have begun
  And have tried,
The very sight of man to shun
  With pride.

I smile before a fresh-dug tomb
  That warns me I must die :
I dread not Tophet's mystic gloom,
  Nor feel shy—
To sniff of crypts the stale perfume,
  Not I !

The sight of priest I scoff and flout
  Despite of hoary years,
His woollen cowl, and mouldy clout,
  And false tears
Will not protect his holy snout
  From jeers !

Death would I welcome with delight
    If my soul on its wing
Could change to viper's fangs in flight
    And could spring—
On earth again—for snakes can bite
    And sting—

"I F."

OH beauty fond and fair!
    Of thy hair—
The comb I fain would be.
    When o'er thy moulded arms,
    And thy charms;
Falls the soft silken sea.

Why am I not the veil—
    Light and frail,
Masking thy eyes' mild ray?
    Or perfumed by the sip
    Of thy lip—
The flower thou throw'st away?

Why am I not the dove,
    Cooing love—
Fondled upon thy breast?
    Or else the breezelet fanned—
    By thy hand,
To cool thy ardent zest?

If I were but thy ring,
  I would cling—
Fast to thy finger white :
  And I would softly press,
    And caress—
The dimpled flesh each night.

How I would love to be,
  Small and wee—
Thy gaiter, ribbon-tied !
  Or thy sheets, white and sleek
    —As thy cheek :
Which thy fair bosom hide.

Or better still I deem—
  The sweet dream,
That lifts thy pulsing spheres,
  For here my flame could burn
    And could learn
My heart's vague hopes and fears.

LIFE.

'Tis for some a grand poem of pleasure,
  'Tis for poets a poem of pain ;
And for others a scintillant treasure,
  A blessing a curse or a bane :
'Tis for many a ramble and leisure,
  And for some 'tis a thing of disdain.

There is ever the failure of trying,
  And the swarms of vague manifold fears;
There's the farce of our birth and our dying,
  The burlesque of our wretched careers.
There is little of value save sighing,
  There is nothing of worth but our tears!

There are false joys, and riches, ambition,
  There is Love, there is Fame, there is Art,
Ere we grapple them, comes inanition,
  Death's shadows can everything part—
All our life-aims are aims of perdition,
  And with hopes that are hopeless we start.

Wise is he who a man and a chooser
  Spurns Life's book and its pages of days,
Wise is he who is no man's accuser,
  Who laughs not, nor sings not, nor prays,
Wise is he who sees all like a muser
  Through vague tenebrous shadows of greys.

Be content and live on nothing claiming,
  Shun the mass and their impotent creeds,
See with eye neither lauding nor blaming,
  Acts of crime, or magnificent deeds,
Neither asking, nor hoping, nor aiming,
  For joys that are barren of seeds.

If we lived through long epochs and ages,
  If we saw but a century of peace,
Had we time to calm murmurs and rages,
  Had we time to make wickedness cease,
We might barter our faith to the sages,
  We might force evil thoughts to decrease.

But we live but an hour and we learn not
  If that hour will be short or be long ;
Shall we rush on ahead, shall we turn not,
  Shall our voice be a sigh or a song?
Shall we love not, nor hate not, nor spurn not
  Who can guide to the right from the wrong?

Can we live without error or blunder,
  Can we know when to come and to go?
Why love, when Death's sickle asunder
  Cleaveth down ev'ry love with a blow?
If the spring turns to winter why wonder,
  Or if roses give way to the snow?

Every sunset in colorful glory,
  Must bow to the menacing night,
Every moon in its opal sheen, hoary,
  Is chased by the dawn's kiss of white,
From chaos there sprang but one story—
  Our story of ruin and blight !

Can we aught of the infinite borrow,
  Can we plunge in the secrets of glooms?
Can we unveil the formless to-morrow,
  Can we sniff at the future's perfumes ?
Can we say that in joy or in sorrow
  We will reach the pale portals of tombs?

Yet like lost lambs, wolf-scented, we tremble ;
  We know not, yet would know and groan ;
We worship our gods and assemble—
  In temples of marble and stone ;
We pray, hope, fear, lie, and dissemble,
  Yet we err through Life's vortex alone !

So is wise he who nothing remembers,
　　Who can banish, forget, and ignore:
Who can crush out the slow-burning embers—
　　Of fire-thoughts that burned well in yore,
Who alike blends the Mays with Decembers,
　　Who cares naught of the past to restore.

Wise is he who regrets not his gladness,
　　His blisses of childhood now dead:
Wise is he who can laugh at his madness—
　　When youth's ardor ruled heart and ruled head:
Wise is he who finds pleasure in sadness,
　　In the memories of tears that were shed.

GLAMOUR.

A BLOND pale moonbeam falls
　　Athwart a window's sill:
　　Soft shimmering on the still—
White gloss of marble walls. . . . .

Frail atoms of white light
　　Sing in an argent glow—
　　White songs of sheen and snow,
White melodies,—dream white. . . . .

Of richest agate wrought,
　　That palace window holds—
　　A gem of silks and golds,
Japan's fair Empress,—fraught—

With whims of flowers and birds,
  Companions of her home ;
  Sweeter heart-fancies roam—
So vague they have no words. . . .

Upon great grees of gold,
  On pillars gemmed of crest,
  On molten silver, prest—
In stairways, jasper-cold.

On fountains, pearls of work,
  Chiselled with arabesque,
  Where images grotesque
'Neath strange devices lurk.

On Kiosks whence breezes blow
  Rich redolent perfumes,
  Luxurious in the glooms
Of porticoes below—

The Empress jewel-clad
  Gazes: and lowly sighs. . . . .
  She turns two lustrous eyes
Up to the white moon sad—

For hours she courts its glare,
  Red lips ope—half apart,
  Soft beats a moon-thrilled heart—
Why does she linger there?

Because the moon's bright beams
  Fall on the window's sill,
  And in the dark night, still,
Tell their white wondrous dreams. . . . . . .

GODS OF FEAR.

TO . . . .

No dainty cooings will I use
    Thy love to win.
Thy virgin faith will ne'er abuse,
And no glib phrases can accuse—
    A lie held in.
Thy Love shall sprout from flowers of Fear
A Love all Passion and all Fear
    Pricking thy skin—

I'll lead thee when the tempests howl
    Within the glade:
To shudder at the hoot of owl,
And laugh to see thee 'neath its scowl—
    Shrink sore afraid.
When livid glares of lightning gleam,
When winds and waves and ravens scream
    Through shadeless shade—

I'll lead thee in the forests deep
    Each ghoulish night:
The fern a lullaby will keep
While on an orchal-mound wilt sleep,
    A sleep of fright—
Moon-ravished, will thy hot veins freeze
Thy sweat will mix with dew of trees
    The Earth's tears, white. . . .

By horror thou wilt love me, when
        Lost in some swamp:
We wallow through the sizy fen,
Fleeing the poisoned shade of glen,
        As we ramp—
Mid spraints and vipers, fungus-bred,
And putrid mushrooms, ochre-red
        Stenchful and damp—!

Down in dank crypts where lizards reign
        Where coffins rest:
I'll desecrate the bodies, slain—
By leprosy, or ulcerous pain,
        And purple pest.
To show thee how the vermine crawl
And how stale carrion can appal
        Thy reaching breast.

In dungeons dark as hearts that hate,
        Thy hand in mine:
I'll lead thee to behold the fate
Of marcid sufferers, who wait—
        Wan-faced, and pine,
For Death or Light with maniac trust,
As o'er foul swill, or fouler crust
        They pain-drunk, whine!

Then, shouldst thou spurn my offers, quake
        And rend thy hair!
The "Gods of Fear" thy life will make—
A hell of hells, asleep, awake,
        Here, yon, or there—
While flameful eyes, with blood for lights
Will show thee other direr sights
        To rock despair!— —

FABLE.

A ROSE-BUSH in a garden grew,
   On which a modest bud had spread
Its virgin fragrance, while the dew
   In drops of pearl had kissed the red—
Soft mantling blush of petals new
   And wond'ring, while the bud was fed
By amorous sunbeams, mild of hue,
   And cautious, lest the rose should dread
Too fulvid glares from skies too blue.

A grovelling worm beneath had seen
   The rose, and hated it for all—
Its gentle charm, though odors keen
   And subtle, would arise and fall
To perfume all the worm's sad spleen :
   Ungratefully this worm did crawl
Up to the tender bud, between—
   Its creamy leaflets, leaving gall,
To blight its helplessness serene.

Venomed and soiled by kissings tart,
   The floweret faded 'neath its woes :
No dew could heal the slayer's smart,
   No thorn the passage could oppose.
Its chalice eaten part and part,
   It perished, and its dying throes
Forced not the abject worm to start—
   Thou wert that beauteous virgin rose,
I was the worm that gnawed thy heart !

PERLINE.

On the sun-kisst sands,
On the golden sands,
Where the argent sea-foams play.—
In the fertile lands,
In the happy lands,
Of the far and fair Cathay:
I wooed a water-Fay—

On the willing waves,
On the magic waves,
She allured my heart away—
In the Ocean's caves,
In the shell-built caves,
I lived and I loved a day:
My beauteous water-Fay—

Where the billows rose,
Where the blue tides rose,
I was cradled by her lay—
Where the alga grows,
Where the sea-plant grows,
Where the scaly mermaids play—
I kissed my water-Fay.

As a moonbeam white,
As a starbeam white,
Was her eye of iris ray—

As a meteor bright,
As a comet bright,
Was her smile of pearl and spray:
Entreating me to stay—

She sighed when I said,—
She swooned when I said,—
That no more could I delay;
That they thought me dead,—
That they mourned me dead,—
In the far and fair Cathay:
And I left my water-Fay—

She wept in my hands,
She sobbed in my hands,
When I sadly swam away—
On the golden sands,
On the sun-kisst sands,
Two pearls in my wet palms lay:
The tears of my water Fay!

TO MY FRIEND EDGAR FAWCETT,

FROM the ruin and rust of ages,
   From the chaos of formless spheres :
From all Pains that Pain assuages,
   From all pangs of endless years :
To our world of sins and rages,
   Thou hast come to stay our fears.
       Giant—defiant.
     Oh Poet of Tears !

And those tears are strong and splendid,
   As the thoughts that make them flow ;
For their riot flood is blended,
   With a smile that lurks below:
And the tears have scarcely ended—
   When we see the smile's deep glow.
       Beautiful ; dutiful :
     Oh Poet of Woe !

Thy verse is not all of gladness
   Of this world so full of stain :
It is lit by a gleam of madness—
   A vague flicker of proud disdain :
And thy lays have a tinge of sadness ;
   Like blue skies before a rain.
       Frigid : rigid.
     Oh Poet of Pain !

Are thy pains more sweet than thy pleasures?
　Is thy sting or thy balm the most cold?
Oh grand soul-rousing genius that measures
　All the glories of dream-thoughts untold—
To lavish thy mind's gems and treasures,
　On a world that is callous and old!
　　　Hateful, ungrateful:
　　Oh Poet of Gold!

With the pearl and the silk of thy dreaming,
　Thou hast woven a magical thread
Of soft musical tissues o'erteeming—
　With the mem'ries of better things fled:
While the palette of language is gleaming
　And bathes them with colors that wed.
　　　Yellow—mellow—
　　Oh Poet of Red!

Through new by-roads of thought thou hast taken
　Our sense and our soul by the rare—
Subtle sweetness of perfumes, which shaken
　Have weighted with fragrance the care—
Of our rapture, and left us forsaken
　All the strength of thy fancies to bear.
　　　Specious: precious:
　　Oh Poet of Prayer!

For at times thy clear voice is endearing,
　Faith-stirring, pure, holy, yet coy:
Dark cark and its spleen-spirits cheering,
　With those exquisite Hope-words that buoy
Till a soul is refreshed beyond fearing,
　With a freshness no gloom can destroy.
　　　Royal: loyal:
　　Oh Poet of Joy!

May the worlds as they muse and they ponder,
  May the men and the minds thereof,
Praise and cherish, and learn to love fonder
  The proud Eagles of Art above,
That from Heaven are sent to wander
  With beaks of iron, and large hearts of dove.
    Grandly—blandly :
  Oh Poet of Love !

MAY 26, 1873.

VICENZA.

In Vicenza the dark,
Not a light—save the spark
    Of a torch.
With a red sullen flame,
O'er the Duke's crested name
    On his porch.

Through the town not a sound,
Not a soul can be found,
    All is still.
With a low gurgling sigh,
The canal rushes by—
    Swift and chill.

The proud palaces, dim—
In the twilight, stand grim
    In their stone :

While the Duomo's grave bell
Droneth out a deep knell
    Monotone.

The tired wanderer may pace
The sad streets, not a face
    To befriend:
And it seems, that the gloom,
Like the life beyond tomb,
    Has no end.

Old Vicenza is dead,
Its past glories have fled,
    And they seem—
Like the memories faint,
Which no mind can paint
    Of a dream!

WHICH?

THERE is one that I could marry—
    Most beautiful to behold:
She must wonder why I tarry,
    But my heart for her is cold—
        For she loves gold.

There is one with cheeks like peaches—
    With large lustrous eyes alert:
Her hair to her ankle reaches,
    But her charms leave me unhurt—
        She loves to flirt.

There is one of lineage olden—
    With a crested, princely name :
Her ringlets are ambry golden,
    But my heart she cannot claim—
        For she loves fame.

There is one with raven tresses—
    With a hot and Spanish skin :
She is lavish of caresses,
    But her heart I spurn to win—
        For she loves sin.

There's another beauty, slender—
    And as supple as a glove :
But for her my heart is tender,
    And as constant as a dove—
        For she loves Love.

CARRION.

FLEEING the city's noisy sound,
    I wandered once oppressed by care
Into the silent woods ; and found
    A naked corpse left rotting there !

Blind with disgust, yet moved by awe,
    I trembling neared the fetid mass ;
Which purple-tinged, and sick'ning raw—
    Exhaled stale wafts of tainted gas.

The eyes by ravenous birds were plucked
　Out of their putrid sockets—while
Eftlets and lizards drained and sucked,
　Their palling food of festered bile—

The rot-gnawed flesh off either cheek
　Hung loose ; and venomed by its stench
The air, which echoed with the shriek
　Of vultures greedy thirst to quench.

A broiling sun with flamant rays,
　Poured down its fulgor through the glade
And by the fervor of its blaze—
　Huge pustules on the carrion made !

A grizzled toad with clammy tread
　O'ergorged with rank and viscous blood,
Lolled sleepily upon his head
　Half hidden in a pool of mud—

Wire worms and adders curled and crawled
　Round in his belly's vapid must,
In which I spied with gaze appalled,
　A dirk begrimed with muck and rust.

His marcid lips ejected grume,
　While carious tumors lapped his throat :
And stunk of gall, and bubbling spume,
　The rancid food of stunted stoat.—

A jaw wide-stretched as if in keck,
　Gaped to my view each cankered gum—
While o'er his limous chin and neck,
　Oozed fecal drops of curdy scum !

A horrid sight, a loathsome death,
  And yet no nausea felt I then—
No deadly vapors choked my breath:
  No reeking miasms dimmed my ken.

Till night had draped my sight in gloom
  On hands and knees the soil I tore:
To give the mildewed corpse a tomb,
  And hide such filth forevermore.

Veiled in the mysteries of thought,
  Before the grave I pondering stood:
My task was o'er—my home I sought,
  And calm in mind I left the wood.—

*   *   *   *   *   *   *   *

Thou! trust and treasure of my heart,
  Thou! beauteous maiden I adore;
At my strange question do not start—
  For a strange answer I implore.

Death, darling mine, is unforeseen;
  Tell me, if dead, wouldst thou embrace
My livid carcass of gangrene?
  My viscid lips? my rotting face?

Wouldst thou with grief my cold hand press
  When decomposing 'neath my shroud?
Wouldst thou thine agony express
  Before a vast and heartless crowd?

If thou wouldst such a love-proof give,
   Thou noblest of all brides wouldst be ;
For such a love, 'tis Love to live—
   And equal love I'd give to thee !

LINES TO ABSINTHE.

WITH wincing sob, and thrilling yell,
Fiends have shed tears, to form thy spell
   Which fascinates my soul.
Which makes me toll my own death-knell,
Wafts up the sin, I cannot quell—
And lures me on the road to hell—
   With torment as a goal !

Unnerved I kneel at thy command,
How can I e'er thy power withstand ?
   When, by its cheering might—
Vistas of glory bright and grand,
Glimpses of bliss on Eden's strand—
Swifter than by a wizard's wand—
   Loom 'fore my dazzled sight !

How of thy sweets can I e'er tire,
Thy magic sway cease to admire—
   When thy pearl drops of green :
Can by their odor calm my ire,
The loftiest, noblest thoughts inspire—
While for the world's good, I aspire,
   In dreamy realms unseen.

For, quaffing from thy nectar source,
Spurred by the suaveness of thy force
 Of happiness I dream.
My mind floats on in placid course,
I know no sting, I feel no loss—
Believe in naught—scoff at remorse—
 Seek only the supreme.

If weary, from my cark-drugged brain—
Thy potency will banish pain,
 And fill my cup of joy.
Ignore I fear—and feel no strain,
Fierce ecstasies that never wane
In thy dear sweets I seek again
 All flitting hopes to buoy.

And when in fancies born of air
Ungrateful liquid, free from care—
 I sip thy venom dire,
Thou sow'st the seed of death to share
Foul Satan's joy, when young and fair—
Fall reckless in thy tempting snare—
 Oh! green and frozen fire!

Outcast and scourge, my tongue is tame,
I have no strength to say I blame—
 Thy fatal sway o'er me.
Thy griffin claws my soul will claim,
Thy savor brings a life of shame,
To end alas in one of flame
 Torment and agony.

But if in rags my limbs are clad,
And if my face is wan and sad,
    Absinthe, I love thee still!
My heart has not alway been bad,
And though the keen world call me mad—
Naught have I had, to make me glad,
    Save thy delirious thrill!

Need I e'er food? by thee am fed,
Need I a love? 'tis thee I wed,
    My pale and glaucous bride:
And though my nerves be dull as lead
In my clenched hand, alive or dead—
I swear that on my dying bed,
    I'll have thee by my side.

LANDSCAPE.

A MOUNTAIN chain—each snow-bathed peak
    Craggy and shapeful, drinks the mist.
Below the cloud-mark, eagles seek
    Their eyries by the sleet-winds kisst.

Mighty Titanic towers of rock,
    Huge Lylacqs raised by giant hands—
To climb to heaven, and to mock
    The power of God on holy strands—

Lay crushed and sundered, overturned,
   Chaos of granite, earth and stone:
Vast grave preadamite, well earned
   For those who shaped it for a throne.

And when Night, hushful, inks the chain—
   With darkness, then the torrents' roar
Soundeth like giant lungs in pain
   Cursing their God for sins of yore.

The souls and spirits of a race
   Damned for all ages suffer there,
And caged in stone, bereft of grace,
   Await their judgment with despair.

SIERRA NEVADA, December, 1872.

LANDSCAPE.

A SETTING sun begilds the sand,
   The pink-tipped wavelets fall and rise,
Murmurless, as the rays expand—
   Their gold-streaked splendor through the skies.

A beach of shells and oolites rare,
   Receives the Ocean's cool embrace:
Above, the ospray cleaves the air,
   Soaring with curves of febrile grace.

No cot, no sward, no trace of man
  No passing sail to intervene:
Blue billows far as eye can scan,
  Red heavens floating o'er the scene.

LANDSCAPE.

In the wood all is still,
    Save the shrill—
Dismal caw of the crow.
  Not a twiglet that stirs,
    And the firs—
Stand out gaunt tipped with snow.

On the road far adown,
    Toward the town—
Not a light, not a sound ;
  White on white, fall the flakes
    On the lakes—
There is rime on the ground.

Twilight fadeth away
    Ashy gray—
The black streaks of Night loom—
  Their dark shadows of void,
    And cloud-buoyed—
Cover all with their gloom.

Dreaded winter appears
Robed in fears:
With its frost and its chill—
While the earth seems to moan
Left alone—
With its rigorous will.

Shunned by all, in despair,
Should I care—
If the autumn has fled?
For my life is as blank
And as dank—
As the sky overhead.

LANDSCAPE.

SUN-REDDENED, brown, a sea of sand
'Neath cloudless skies' white floating heat,
Rolls its grain-waves through Soudan's land,
O'er desert miles no eye can mete.

Mountains of dust arise and loom—
Their scorching shadows on the waste:
To brave the hell-touch of simoum
A caravan prepares in haste . . .

The groaning camels, laden, kneel.
The timorous Bedouins veil their eyes . . .
Torrents of sand from heaven reel—
And pour their heat from hotter skies.

Near by, a source, a palmy mound,
   Oasis of delight is viewed :
Cool bubbling waters kiss the ground,
   Tall date-trees offer shade and food.

*   *   *   *   *   *   *   *

But all around is dry and sere
   As hearts from whence all love has flown :
The heart's oasis still sincere
   Striveth to cheer its life and own :
The sand-whirl passes—'tis too late—
   The martyr-Bedouins die in pain :
E'en tottering towards salvation's gate,
   A love-burnt heart ne'er smiles again.

LANDSCAPE.

A sky of flame ; the Ganges scorched—
   Sluggish and rippleless lolls by :
Marvels of stone, pillared and porched,
   Thrust their pied cupolas on high.

Almées of eye k'hol-tinted, dance—
   A mantling whirl beneath a palm,
Where cloyed inert in haschisch trance
   A bronze-skinned rajah tempteth calm.

With garb striated, black as ink,
  Two Delhi virgins fan with zest,
The musing prince, whose senses sink—
  In promised dreams of Zendavest.

The Kussir's melody, rich, deep
  Filleth with song the arid air:
Cradled by rocking rhythms, sleep—
  In hamac frail comes unaware.

The kaat and sherbet palate-soft,
  Tip his hot tongue with cool surprise,
An ombrel shades, while far aloft
  The attar-gulls' sharp perfumes rise.

The subtle fragrance charms the birds—
  Gold-feathered, as they bless its sweet;
And warble unknown graceful words
  Rhyming with Sun, with Scent, with Heat. . . .

SOUVENIRS.

THE night in June.
The silv'ry moon.
The linnet's cry.
The cobalt sky:
The night when first we met
  Can you forget?

The forest green.
The liquid sheen.
The dripping oars.
The sudden pause—
That silent sweet duet,
    Can you forget?

The brilliant ball.
The crowded hall.
The blaze of light.
The kiss that night.
The night you called me pet.
    Can you forget?

The jingling bells.
The snow-clad dells.
The speeding sledge.
The solemn pledge.
The pledge you made coquette.
    Can you forget?

The serenade.
The leafy glade.
The pouring rain.
The hurricane.
The night my lips were wet.
    Can you forget?

The lonely park.
The shadows dark.
The first caress.
The silken tress.
This, ravishing brunette,
    Can you forget?

12

The vow of love.
The glance above.
The ardent thrill—
The power of will—
That hour brought no regret.
    Can you forget?

The dream of bliss.
The parting kiss.
The days glide fast.
The dream is past.
Beauty with eyes of jet,
    You *can* forget!

TO . . .

SLEEP and dream, lissome maid, while in rapture
    I caress thy grand poem of flesh ;
    While I toy with each rich purple mesh
Of gnarled tresses : when striving to capture
    All the hot biting odors from lips—
    Half apart with the sweetness that slips
From thy dimpled white smilings, sleep-fresh.

'Tis the perfect round curve of thy shoulder,
    And thy sleek supple flanks I admire.
    For thy moonish-white skin doth inspire
My hot, vexed, restless gaze to pierce bolder;
    For thou sleepest, and red is thy dream
    With the naphtha of lust, and its gleam
From the snows of thy breast hurls its fire.

Nay, awake not, nor turn, till I press thee,
   For thy sleep is consoling as Night.
   And thy calm dreams shall taste the fire-might
Of Love's blendings, as mad, I caress thee,
   And thy white form with red kisses mark—
   Till thine eyes wake from lethargies dark—
To the glamours and splendors of light.

Then from dream-bliss to Life-bliss arisen,
   Thine hot tears, my hot tears will dispute,
   Then thy low pant sounds softer than lute
To my ear; and thy bare arms imprison—
   A no longer wild phantom of sighs,
   For thou closest thy large blurrèd eyes,
And liest wond'ring, nude, pallid, and mute!

Let my kisses then follow incessant,
   O'er thy lips, o'er thy soft cheek of fur:
   Let them moisten, as sultry they err
The black shade of thy silken brows' crescent—
   While I breathe the mysterious air,
   From thy chaos of undulate hair,
Vague and dreamy as memories of myrrh.

BLUE.

An azure smile the Heavens wear,
  A broad grand smile, intensely blue.
The turquoise tint has dyed the air—
  The breeze seems colored by its hue . . . . .

Cerulean blue, the sea below—
  Lies like the mirror of the sky:
Its blue is of a richer glow,
  Its changings wondrous to the eye.

The maid I love hath orbs of blue,
  A melting blue, faith-lit by me:
Her steadfast sapphire glancings, true—
  Have gulfs of cobalt harmony.

Once sailed we o'er the blue blue seas,
  Scudding beneath far bluer skies:
And worlds of Blue, on bended knees,
  I found within her loving eyes.

TOURS.

With lambent flow—
The Sun aglow
Caresses, gair, with waves of light,
A church's painted windows, white—
With rime and snow.

Glass-carvèd, quaint—
Each haloed saint
With wrinkled trailing mantle blue,
Blends soft with tints of antique hue
Holily faint.

Through fissured spire,
The sunbeam's gyre,
Weaveth a magic web of rays—
Iris, gold-gleaming as it plays—
On marbled choir—

Long, dark, severe,
The naves appear
In pious patriarchal gloom:
Circled by columned walls, that loom
Their shades austere.

The Sun's proud glare
To lume a prayer
Ne'er penetrates the tombs of stone:
Far chillier when the organ's moan—
Rendeth the air.

But once each day
A wand'ring ray
Lustres the chapel's sculptured domes,
Over the pillared transept roams,
Then fades away.

Its warmth is chilled,
Its calor stilled,
The stern cold grandeur of the mass—
Seems to resent its right to pass,
And shuns it, thrilled—

By grief and tear,
My heart—joy-sere
Slumbers in darkness like that aisle,
For no fair sunbeam can beguile,
Or reach to cheer !

Care-lost, in dreams—
It seeth streams
Of splendent sunlight on the walls :
Cruelly deaf to anguished calls
For paltry beams.

The days begun,
Die one by one
While sad that heart in silence weeps,
As on and on the Life-tide creeps
Bringing no sun.

But once each day
A pitying ray,
Cheers the poor heart with sorrow fraught,
Warms it awhile with kindly thought,
Then fades away . . . .

Tours, October, 1872.

BALLAD.

If the sky be pure,
  Take care !
If the road seem sure,
  Beware !
Let no maid allure
  Though fair.

Of the hand of king,
  Take care !
If the thrushes sing,
  Beware !
False is every thing
  And e'er . . .

If a friend appears,
  Take care !
Of a woman's tears,
  Beware !
If an old man jeers,
  Despair !

Of the shade of priest,
   Take care!
Of the hoof of beast,
   Beware!
And an offered feast
   Ne'er share.

Of varlets and thieves,
   Take care!
Of venom in leaves,
   Beware!
Of a breast that heaves
   Half bare . . . .

If an eye be blue,
   Take care!
If 'tis black of hue,
   Beware!
No color is true
   Of glare.

Of a damsel's kiss,
   Take care!
Of the serpent's hiss—
   Beware!
If thou seekest bliss,
   'Tis rare.

So of stars and sun,
   Take care!
If the field is won,
   Beware!
And all mortals shun
   As snare.

ESMERALDA.

In dreams I saw a sprite,
    Pearly white.
    Gazing by my side—
    Bathing in a tide—
    Of soft light,
As flitting moonbeams plied.

World of quiescent grace
    Was her face :
    Saintly was her mien—
    Tranquil and serene—
    And no trace
Of sin or guile was seen.

Long, and of golden glare
    Was her hair;
    Trailing to the ground—
    Hiding as it wound—
    From my stare
Her moonèd spheres so round.

Rapt, lay I in a trance
    By her glance ;
    Flashing forth to gleen—
    Flashing chill and keen—
    As a lance
Argent tinged, and green.

Of no pale glaucous tint
 Was their glint
 Luscious green, and deep—
 Like a lake at sleep—
 And no stint
On yearnings could I keep.

Eager, strove I to press
 And caress—
 Blinded by delight—
 Dazzled by the sight—
 Of each tress
Gairish blonde and bright.

The tempting houri sped
 When the red
 Fulgid nacker ray—
 Warned her it was day:
 And with dread
She vanished in dismay.

Her last and parting gaze
 Was of praise:
 Smaragd, arched by jet
 Tender, passion wet—
 And its blaze
On Earth I'm seeking yet.

KISSES.

There's a kiss of nature charming,
  The fond mother's kiss to her child :
The babe's fancied fears disarming,
  By the touch of her lips, so mild—
That visions of sleep, alarming
  Fade fast from its mind beguiled.

A kiss that ignoreth reason,
  Is the kissing of roused desire—
'Tis blind to a future treason,
  And does naught of the past inquire:
For the spice of lust in season—
  Has the heat and the strength of fire.

There's a kiss of noble pleasure,
  The lover's kiss to his bride.
An embrace that hearts can treasure,
  With feelings of joy and of pride:
Till later, those hearts can measure,
  The full flood of the marriage tide—

There's a kiss as warm and winning
  To the sense, as golden wine—
'Tis the kiss of love beginning,
  For whose magic lips pout and pine:
God pardons the bliss of sinning,
  For its essence is right divine—

There's a kiss, the kiss of parting,
    An unwelcome sad embrace:
When unchecked tears are darting,
    O'er a pallid anxious face—
As the moment nears for starting,
    O'er treacherous seas and worlds of space.

There's a kiss of anguish horrid,
    When Death comes to claim its prey:
When blanchened are cheeks once florid,
    When mourners kneel round, and pray:
That kiss on a chilly forehead,
    When a loved life ebbs away.

SONNET.

I FAIN would find the home my sorrows crave,
    A rocky shelter in some chill still spot:
    Live, cenobite estranged, within a grot—
Near sombrous firs; where alpine tempests rave—
With roots to suck, and hot raindrops to lave
    My thirst; secluded, would I live and rot
    In drugget foul, glad in my chosen lot—
Though still a boy, to tamper with the grave!
Learn what I know, know what I learned and sought,
Plough through the sterile wilderness of thought,
Muse on the myriad mysteries of old,
    Curse every day and hope 'twill be my last,
Dream o'er my wishful life, its dreams of gold,
    Dream of Eternity—and of the past! . . . .

LANGUAGE.

THERE is a language I have heard in dreams
   Whispered by formless clouds, by ouph and gnome,
   Sound that like water breaking into foam
With sad unearthly song and music teems:
An idiom unctuous like oil in streams,
Full of grand mellow words like "star," like "Rome!"
Such as cannot in any cobwebbed tome
Of antique lore be found; whose carol quemes,
Subtle of strain like rich sonorous Zend
Full of strange syllables that have no end. . . . .
A tongue wherein low liquid echoes swell
   Of worlds unknown ; which mortals cannot speak
Something like velvet crushed upon a bell . . . .
   Something like amorous sighs, or murmured Greek!

NEGRA VENUS.

ZAZZA, fair pompous-breasted perfect queen
   A marvellous glory of black flesh thou wert. . . .
Vast, sdainful seas now oscillate between
   Our early loves; although, by age unhurt,
   Time-scorning, still my faithful mind alert
Recalls the splendors of thy regal mien,

Thy supple body, perfumed, hot, ungirt
Reposing hamac-lulled, slave-fanned, inert,
Where towering high above, palmettos green
Shaded thy nubile form from sun-thrusts keen.

Can I forget thy velvet-ebon skin,
   Thy torse, grace flexile, and thine eyes
Mirage of sultry prisms, flashing in—
   And out, like fulg'rous lightning through dark skies?
   That face, like Greece's Phryne's, praise defies;
For thou wert grandly black ! and must be kin
   To Night, whose spirit robed thee in its dyes
   Densest:—when white-skinned born, thou fell'st its
         prize,
And by its kissings, thou of Venus twin
To black wert turned : sign of thy mystic sin.

Can I forget thy coast, fair Zanzibar,
   Deluged in gold, in verdure, and in light ?
And thou my proud browed queen, can aught debar
   Or check my longings for thy sunny might ?
   Well I revive the day, the hour, the site
When in the umber shadows from afar
   I saw thee hast'ning through the jealous Night :
   While from thy burnished body black and bright
Thou threw'st aside thy scarlet veil-cymàr
Masking the raptures of thine eyes' black star.

Ah ! I adore the sweets of things that were,
   The red lust-loves, the deep black loves of Dream,
The music of thy fire-throat's Afric purr,
   The wonders of thy dusky eyes' wild gleam :
   Whose magic twinklings, radiant, would redeem
The sins and vilest crimes of souls that err

In deepest Hells: and I, while mem'ries teem,
Recall each scorching kisses' pang supreme.
Kisses like sweet, sad, subtle scents of myrrh,
Kisses rich, soft and sensuous, like fur.

May 19, 1873.

SPLEEN.

ALL the strength of my soul thou corrodest,
   Thou hast woven a raiment of blight
For my shoulders that bend as thou loadest
   My body with burdens of fright:
And by spirits of horror thou goadest
   My soul into oceans of night !—

Thou hast shrivelled a cheek that was florid
   With thy murmurous voice of despair;
Thou hast kindled hell fires that torrid
   Have burned my vitality bare,
And the wrinkles that mark a young forehead
   I owe to thy vigilant care.

All the art-loves and song-loves of beauty,
   All the musings of things great and grand,
All the splendors of justice and duty,
   Thou hast cleft with thy poisonous wand:
While my life is thy prey and thy booty
   And thy hot claws my talent have spanned.

Thou hast shattered each hope-pillared palace
  I built in my fond youthful dream ;
Thou hast ruined with truculent malice
  A mind wherein word-glories teem ;
Thou hast left but a cloud-spirit callous,
  Where once shone a soul-spirit's beam.

Thou hast changed all my songs into sadness,
  All the gold of my thoughts into brass :
Thou hast wept and hast whined o'er my gladness
  For the arts or the loves of a lass ;
Thou hast driven me down into madness
  To the level of brutes and the mass.

So accomplish thy fiend work, destroy me,
  Pray lavish thy dose of gangrene :
But cease to revile and annoy me
  With tauntings so merciless keen :
Strike coreward, kill, stifle, o'ercloy me,
  And damn me in torrents of spleen !

BALLAD.

Men in mail,
  Crowd the hall!
To my tale,
  Listen all.
Knights and lords—
Sheathe your swords—
Cease discords—
  Slave and thrall.

Courtly dames,
  Hasten near,
Leave your games,
  Lend an ear.
For my song—
If not long—
Will prolong—
  Our good cheer.

And to-night,
  Quoth the King;
Dreams of fright,
  Will I bring.
On the Rhine—
Starlets shine—
O'er our wine—
  Let us sing.

13*   145

'Tis the time,
  And the hour ;
In quaint rhyme,
  Hearts to cower.
Listen well—
While I tell—
Of the bell—
  In the Tower.

In the old—
  Time by gone ;
A right bold—
  Lord high born,
Steel arrayed—
With sharp blade—
Wooed a maid—
  One bright morn.

She was frail,
  She was fair—
And was pale,
  As her hair.
Which was gray—
As the ray—
Of dawn day—
  Blonde and gair.

And her eyes
  Were as blue,
As the skies'
  Cobalt hue.

While her arms—
And her charms—
Brought alarms—
  To man's view.

The brave Knight,
  Passion-fanned,
Of this sprite
  Sought the hand.
And did grieve—
I believe—
Till Yule Eve—
  In the land.

It is said
  In the lay,
They were wed
  On Christ's day.
In strange tongue—
Poets sung—
Love! ye young—
  Now, alway.

The fair bride
  Of the Knight,
By his side
  Robed in white:
Seemed to grin—
O'er a sin—
Held within—
  With delight.

O'er a feast
   Spread with craft,
Mirth increased,
   Guests had laughed.
Golden wine—
Juice divine—
Rich and fine—
   Had been quaffed.

Sudden rang
   With a knell,
The deep clang
   Of a bell!
And its thrill—
Sent a chill—
Which no will—
   Could e'er quell.

In the hall
   From affright,
One and all
   Rose outright.
Who has power—
In the Tower—
At this hour—
   Cried the Knight!

As he smote
   On his shield,
The bell's throat
   Echo reeled

Grim and dire—
As the fire—
Of God's ire—
  It repealed !

Said the host,
  There's a spell,
Or a ghost
  In that bell.
For its zeal—
My cold steel—
It shall feel—
  Long and well.

Unappalled,
  Anger-rife,
He now called
  For his wife.
To embrace—
Her sweet face—
Fair with grace—
  'Fore the strife.

But the dame
  Thus implored
Never came
  To her lord.
She had flown—
All alone—
From her throne—
  At the board.

The Castel
   Heard with fear
The deep bell
   Ring out clear,
And its boom—
Like the gloom—
Of the tomb—
   Awed the ear.

'Tis the din,
   Said the Knight,
Of a Djinn
   Or a sprite.
I will go—
And will show—
What a blow—
   I can smite.

The bell chimed
   Its dull blare
As he climbed
   The tower stair,
Bat and owl—
Fetid foul—
Ceased to scowl—
   'Neath his stare.

And each guest
   With a will,
Hoped his test
   He would fill.

And that blood—
Thick as mud—
In a flood—
   He would spill.

Ev'ry light
   Low had burned,
But the Knight
   Ne'er returned,
And till late—
Did friends wait—
Till his fate—
   Could be learned.

Vassals sought
   The Castel,
And news brought
   Of the bell.
Which still rung—
Where it hung—
Its iron tongue—
   And its knell.

The Knight bound
   On the floor,
They had found
   In his gore!
His limbs strained—
His head brained—
His breast drained—
   To the core.

By his side,
    Pale and mute,
Sat his bride,
    Ghoul-like brute.
And she sucked—
Blood bemucked—
And hair, plucked—
    By the root.

The guests fled
    In dismay,
And 'tis said
    In the lay
The bell swings—
The ghoul rings—
And she sings—
    To this day.

The King's song
    And its rhyme,
Creeps along
    To our time.
The same bell—
Is known well—
In the dell—
    Bergenheim.

GRIPSHOLM.

In a lonely site,
Where the restless white—
Sad waves of Lake Mälar play,
For ages alone,
An old kirk of stone,
Has stood in its solitude cold and gray,
With its steeple shaped like the letter A.

When the twilight falls,
Its shadow appals,
So mystic and grim it seems :
While none can control
From his inner soul
Fears chilling and vague as the fears of dreams
When that church is lit by the moon's pale beams.

When the nights are dark,
Far above a spark—
From the belfry darts its ray.
Where a white owl sits
And perches, and flits,
From the midnight toll, to the dawn of day,
In the little old steeple like an A.

And its hoot is sad
Like the echo mad
Of some plaintive spirit strain,

14   153

And its eyes like fire
From the olden spire
Shine lurid through sleet through snow and rain,
With a fierce gleam tinged as if by pain.

It ceases to grieve
When on cold Yule eve
The peasants come in to pray ;
And it seems to gloat
When the iron throat—
Of the great bell haileth the Saviour's day,
Far up in the steeple like an A.

For it sits all night
Stern, solemn, and white
And its dismal hoot is stilled :
While it listens there
To the evening prayer
And winks as in joy of some wish fulfilled
While the timorous peasants watch it, thrilled.—

And they murmur low
That in years ago
The kirk's first bishop was slain :
In the graveyard's gloom
You can see his tomb,
But his angered soul comes to earth again
Till the murderer by his side be lain.

And they draw more near
As they tell in fear
How they heard their mothers say ;

That the lonely owl
With the great white scowl
Was the soul of the bishop who used to pray
In that kirk with the steeple like an A.

LA BELLE IMPÉRIA.

Une desconficture d'hommes ne lui coustoyt qu'ung gentil soubrire.—
BALZAC.

In the quaint olden city of Tours,
   In the good year twelve hundred and ten,
   There assembled most wonderful men,
Knights and prelates, monks, margraves and boors,
   Famous sages and thinkers of ken,
Gallant minstrels and gay troubadours.

The old cardinal-soldier Raguse,
   And the portly old bishop of Coire ;
   Men of mitre of crown and of lyre—
Men whose name no vile scribe could accuse,
   Came in brilliant and grotesque attire
In their cassocks of silk, and vair-shoes.

The fat abbots in drugget and clout,
   Their round bellies o'erfilled with good cheer :
   All the vassals and footmen of spear,
All the jesters with quip and with shout,
   All the warriors with steel-woven gear,
All the people of frolic about—

Used to gather within the arcade
  In the quaint and the picturesque street
  Where the Flower of Touraine used to greet
The assembly of wit and of blade,
  Where Impéria the peerless would meet—
All her guests in their splendor arrayed.

Where silk, velvet, and satin were spread
  In luxurious lavish and pride ;
  Where the palace's portals oped wide—
To the throng of young gallants who led—
  Through the corridors, women who vied
In their radiance with stars overhead !

Where strange coifs and odd costumes would blend
  With the glitter of casque and of shield :
  Where the hauberk and buckler gold-steeled—
Would shine midst the dames who would bend—
  Their lace head-dresses prone as they kneeled
On Impéria's throne ere ascend—

Here the laughter, the mirth, and the song—
  Swelled in music tumultuous and gay,
  Here from vespers till coming of day
Did the revellers orgies prolong ;
  With the joys of the cup, and the lay—
Of the troubadour chanting his wrong—

From great goblets of richly-wrought gold
  With the arms and device of Touraine,
  Did the guests tope and empty and drain—
The rich wines of Navarre, strong and old,
  Till the corridors echoed again
With their shouts and the tales that they told.

On her throne Queen of beauty and charm
   Sat Impéria the fairest of all,
   While above her on oaken glossed wall—
Hung great weapons of torment and harm ;
   Mammoth glaives to be carried on spall,
Swords and daggers whose sight brought alarm.

And Bordeaux's great Archbishop to right
   Stood to serve her with sweets, and with wine;
   Baudricourt the scarred hero malign,
At her left showed and strutted his might,
   While about her shone jewels divine—
While around her shone splendors of light !

Never sovereign had handsomer court,
   Never Queen had more thralls or more gems,
   For they clustered like grapes to the hems—
Of her satin robes, fretted and wrought—
   With brocade, gold and huge diadems
Each one given for love and not bought.

Great carousal and wassail she said
   Is the victor and soother of time !
   Sing ye bards in your happiest rhyme,
Would she cry as she smiled white and red—
   With a birdlike coy motion sublime,   .
'Tis the hour to be gay and to wed—

And the poets would warble again
   For soft music can sorrows dispel :
   And while rebec, lute, cithern, would swell—
In sweet unison ! goldenest rain
   Whether angelot, crown, or agnel,
Would be tossed by the proud Castellaine.

Then the noble de Coucy rose up
   Stung to quick by some haughty remark ;
   There was danger and death in the spark—
Of his eye, as he hurled his gold cup—
   At proud Sigismond, Baron of Arcque,
When he told him like swine he did sup !

And with feverous strength he unsheathed
   His long rapier of damascened steel :
   Torqued, embossèd in silver, for zeal
By the Spaniards' great emperor bequeathed,
   And he tempesting swore it should feel—
The hot vitals of Arcque as he breathed !

Come laggard he cried, thou hast said
   That Impéria our lucific Queen
   Was a sullen pute, foul and obscene,
And for this thou shalt gasp till art dead :
   While her mercies shall not intervene,
Till my sword by thy blood has been fed.

Thou art oathish and chippy I swear
   Howled the Baron, with menacing eye,
   Say thy Aves and Paters for I
Shall bring thee to thy milk in despair,
   Thou ruffian ! thou bastard ! come try—
To pull blood from the roots of my hair !

And a scabbard I'll make of thine heart
   Proud laird ! while yon lubrical wench
   Shall sniff up thy foul body's dead stench
When my glaive shall have cleft thee in part,
   For the thirst of my ires I will quench
In the loam of thy bile and thy smart— !

Then Impéria the lepid, the fair !
    Smiled demurely and beckoned her page.
    Let these bold cavaliers in their rage—
Unmolested have space and fresh air,
    Clear the vestibule now while they wage
Their combat so glorious and rare.

And when the Knights struggled she laughed,
    And would clap her white hands in delight.
    What I dote on is passionate fight—
Was her cry as she nibbled, and quaffed—
    Sugar-cakes and sweet golden wines, light,
While admiring each Palatin's craft.

For they waxed warm with anger and smote
    With a nerve upon helmet and mail,
    They were tiger-like lithe to assail—
And ward blows from the breast or the throat,
    Till at last loss of blood made them pale,
And the vassals could weariness note.

Neither sued nor for mercy nor rest,
    And continued with shout and with yell
    Till all woundful and gory they fell
All bedabbled with blood on their crest,
    Then Impéria would say " it is well"
Let them die and their deeds shall be blest.

*   *   *   *   *   *   *   *   *

Then the laughter the mirth and the song
    Kept increasing tumultuous and gay,
    When the corpses were carried away
Did the jolly Touringians prolong—
    All the joys of the cup, with the lay
Of the troubadour chanting his wrong.

MOON-MUSIC.

BLOND moonbeams shine in symphonies of light
   Upon the surface of a sleeping lake,
   Blue shadows, deep in dormant depths opaque
Flit under dainty ripples, moonlit, bright,
Around, the myriad voices of the night
   Blend with the moon's vague song, and make
   Wonderful concerts of soft tunes, that break
In foam, in sheen, in toneful soulful flight:
   Sound like the kiss of wave upon a pearl—
   Sound like the flesh-thrill of an amorous girl—
Music so dreamlike subtle, that no ear
   Save that of muser can enjoy its balm,
Sound like the murmur of a falling tear—
   Sound like a twilight hush of endless calm. . .

·

———————

MOONBEAMS.

RECALLEST thou that night
    Of delight,
When the moon in play—
Clad thee oh my fay—
In a silv'ry ray—
    Milky white,
    To ignite
Fires which in thee lay?

Recallest thou the scene
  So serene,
Where we held our tryst—
Where our lips first kissed—
Who could joys resist—
  When the green,
  Bathed in sheen
Gem-like shone through mist !

Recallest thou when nude
  Fancy crude,
How a moonbeam pearled—
From the star-sprent world,
Kissed thy blonde hair, curled—
  As I viewed
  Passion-lewd,
Ringlets half unfurled— !

Recallest thou the hue
  Nacreous blue,
Of thy form so round :
When thy lily-crowned—
Tresses to the ground
  Toucht the dew,
  'Neath the yew
Where we lay arm bound !

What tints of wondrous dye
  The moon's eye,
Darted on thy face :
Silvered by its grace—

While my one embrace—
　　With thy sigh—
　　Rustled by,
Like leaflets whirred through space!

And no skilled artist's brush
　　Could the blush—
　　Copy of thy cheek:
Rosy, tipt with weak—
Frozen moonbeams meek—
　　Mild of flush,
　　White and lush,
Caprice of a streak!

Oh! the grand color, gair
　　Of thy hair,
When the argent stream—
Pouring beam on beam—
Met its fulvous gleam—
　　Trailing fair
　　O'er thy bare
Shoulders curved supreme!

And as thy jet eyes gazed
　　Passion raised,
Humid-ebon, cloyed—
Opaline—o'erjoyed—
Hope and ardor buoyed—
　　Then I crazed
　　Pressed and praised,
Bounding breasts spheroid!

Recallest thou that sweet
Dream complete,
Witnessed by the moon—
God's or Demon's boon—
Won and lost too soon—
Bold yet bleit
Of conceit,
Acmed in thy swoon !

Night of voluptuous pain
Balm of brain,
Nothing can replace—
Nothing can retrace—
Miracles of grace—
Which time's stain
Gnaws in vain,
But never can efface.

SEVILLE, December, 1872.

NIAGARA.

CHAOS and void of worlds preadamite !
  Lylacqs of clouds, Babelian towers of air !
Maëlstroms of seething elements, shade-night,
  Immensities of space, ignescent glare—
Of shifting meteors, dire, terrific, bright !
  Bewildering grandeurs of a rising prayer !
God heard your cries for formful life, and light—
  Pellucid star-sprent Heavens glimmered, fair !
A world was born, vast shapes, grand seas, were fused
  In perfect symmetry, and naught accused

The Lord of folly, save Niagara's land,
　Whose soul rebelled and mocked a gift of mud :
So smote he it with fire-glaive firm of hand,
　The wound brings forth white cataracts of blood !

SONNET.

I. ONCE could weep when women wept ; their tears
　Whether of joy or pain, or love for me
Moved all the meekness of my soul ; for fears,
　And terrene guiles had spared me : I was free
And pure of holiest thought, yet young in years.
　My lips breathed freshness and its sympathy.
The coreless skeleton of Time now leers
　Upon the threshold of my soul. I see—
Callous, indifferent, scenes of blood and crime
　The poor despair, the wicked upward climb,
My trusts in God and youth I long have spurned
　My sinning life-tides slowly Deathward creep,
But oh ! how has my skeptic spirit yearned
　To shed one simple tear when women weep !

ROME.

Ruin and rot their raging rule have rolled
   Rebellions, o'er the glories of thy dead !
Recall not regal dreams of carnage red,
   Revels and triumphs, routs and robes of gold,
Revert no vain regret on splendors fled :
   Rude, rushing time, with rigid, ruthless cold,
Ravishing, reckless, rusts thy royal head ;
   Ravages sanctuaries once rose-souled.
Rest ! in the rank recesses of each dome
Rest ! oh grand town revered, a spirit-home
Ready wilt find when worlds have passed away,
   Regions of air and odorous realms of sky.
Restored in spheres of everlasting day,
   Rome thou shalt never know what 'tis to die !

PERFUME.

When thou art from me, when I cannot glance
   Upon thy rarest beauty, and when mind—
   And soul are panoplied in veils unkind
Of thought forgetful, errant ; when a trance
Dims all my sense, then a sweet spirit grants
   A power to feel thy presence : for I find
   Thine image in strange forms, when musings wind
Coils of aromas, steeped like wines of France

In fragrant vagueness, redolent and sharp ;
Perfumes that bring to mind a soul-thrilled harp,
Odors ecstatic, smells of youth's desire,
    Musk blent with sound, or music heard through hair . .
The scents of breaths that gasp with loveful fire
    Scents of thy loveliness, nude, white, and fair !

SONNET.

TO . . .

I LOVE thine eyes that beckon smiles : two souls
    Radiant with lustres flashing forth grand fires !
    Their opulence of glamour goads desires :
Should sad words murmur, then their glance condoles.
A harmony of tears, heart's manna, rolls—
    Down cheeks disrosed ; until a lip inquires—
    Grief's secrets ; then the first woe-ebb retires
In tranquil tides ; alone, the gaze consoles.
    A smile ! reflection of the soul's bright sun
    Chases all chimeras of pain :—I shun
Dark grooves of palsied thought, becharmed, I look
    And rivet all mine essence in thine eyes,
Vague as the music of a moonbathed brook !
    Vague as great sultry clouds, as twilight skies !

SONNET.

In great grand worlds above, my spirit soars,
  Above our turbid spheres, above in air :
  Roaming insatiate through the planet's glare
To sombrous vales ! to sunless moonless shores !
In cloud-cathedrals prays it—and implores
  The vital virile vim to win the rare—
  Prized benison of reaching regions, where—
The souls of fancy hide their precious stores.
  Above ! above ! errs on my spirit-thought,
  Spurred on to search for things unseen, untaught,
Tremulous, hope-girt, it pursues its flight
  Through skies crepuscular of lurid glow
Bearing back marvels from beyond the Night—
  To feed my mind awaiting them below !

VISION.

Once on a slumbrous languid summer's night,
  I sat content, and courted pleasant dreams ;
  The full moon poured upon me lambent streams
Of glary splendent incandescent light.
And, as my fancy pondered mind-remote,
  I sudden saw from out the sprinkled beams,
(Clad in a trailing robe of ghostly white)
A girlish phantom form emerge and float,
With one great crimson gash upon her throat !

A pallid suffering vision was she, and,
   Direfully paler 'neath that argent moon.
   Eyes had she: startled, like the eyes of loon,
While nervous spasms seemed to twitch her hand.
Hand, small and dimpled, all begemmed, high bred,
   Hair, purplish, wavy, in confusion strewn
Over a youthful bosom, robust, grand—
The deep long throat-wound now profusely bled,
Down on the white robe fell the hot drops, red.

My wondering presence she seemed not to heed,
   Her great eyes trembled in the moon's cold glare,
   I saw her wipe the blood off clotted hair
And then she sighed:—a sigh of utter greed.
Pausing, she spied me without signs of awe,
   And turned her pale sweet face divinely fair
Full on me as if forced by pain or need—
I shuddered, and again unwilling saw
That smooth smooth hideous cut all bleeding, raw . .

A thrill came o'er me, but I did not fear,
   And with quick words of kindness to her spake:
   Assuaging fondnesses to ease her ache:—
Her great vague eyes were moistened by a tear.
But still no answer moved her hueless lip.
   The moonbeams grew more dim, more sad, opaque,
She listened to me with a ravished ear
Advanced, then back into the light would slip,
While still I saw that blood-drain ooze and drip . . .

But as the last pale ray illumed the sill,
   Her poor pale face was shadowed o'er by dread:
   She gazed on me awhile, and bent her head

Close to my throbbing breast, now hot, now chill,
I sighed to rouse the memories of her spleen
    But asked "Whence comes that frightful wound so
        red?"
*   *   *   *   *   *   *   *   *   *
With slow and solemn voice that made me thrill,
She uttered but one word, oh deathlike keen !
That word, that horrid word, was . . . . . guillotine !

WOOD-DREAMS.

ALLEGORICAL.

In a glade I prayed,
   'Neath a giant elm :
And essayed to vade
   In a dreamy realm
   The floods of thought that whelm
A mortal's mind in shade.

The air was by care
   And by sorrow stilled ;
And the glare so gair
   Of the glow-worms, thrilled—
   My lone heart overfilled
By the grandeur of prayer.

The shrill cry and sigh
   Of the winter breeze,
Moaned by in the sky
   Through the cedar-trees,
   While on both bended knees,
My sad gaze erred on high.

And my thought was fraught
　With pious delight,
As I sought and wrought
　In my mind that night,
　The fond chimeras bright
Which the solitude brought.

Yet Hell with its fell
　And malignant power,
Thought well then to quell
　My peace of an hour ;
　And my soul forced to cower
Was o'erawed by its spell.

By my side I spied
　A strange maiden fair :
Who with pride, untied
　Matted fibrous hair,
　And with soft tempting stare,
All my passions defied.

And she gazed, till crazed
　By the wondrous sight
I grew mazed, and dazed
　By her form moon-white ;
　For a sad and wild light
From two deep green eyes blazed.

As I feared, she neared
　The spot where I knelt ;
And appeared and leered
　Till my whole mind felt,
　As if girt by a belt
Of a mystery weird.

On my breast, caressed
  By tresses of gold,
Her lips' zest she pressed
  With vigor untold,
  But her body was cold,
Like a serpent's at rest—

While the green mild sheen
  Of her emerald eyes,
And her mien of queen
  To my soul's surprise
  Caused my ardor to rise
To a height unforeseen.

Like an asp her grasp
  Was sultry and tight,
'Neath her clasp, my gasp
  Rang out in the night
  Half kiss-smothered in flight
By her sting-kiss like wasp.

Then with heat replete
  To possess I yearned,
To eat of her sweet
  The sweet I had spurned :
  While my hot kisses burned
As I fondled her feet.

But the flame of shame
  Lurked not in her eye,
And no name of blame
  In my trance heard I,
  Save the low droning sigh
Of a heart I could claim.

Dream-awake, opaque
  With the sweat of pain,
I now ache to slake
  My passion profane,
  With the sprite, but in vain
'Twas a Lamia, a snake—

Elf-foiled I recoiled
  For the gnomish strife
Fear-spoiled and I boiled
  As I clutched my knife—
  In her bosom Hell-rife
Its carved hilt I blood-soiled.

Through gore to the core
  Of her frame it went,
More, more, foaming sore
  The cold flesh it rent;
  Till beneath me she bent
More appeased than before.

As she bled fear-fed
  In the frantic fray,
Though vim-dead with dread
  Hell called her away,
  And with first light of day
My strange vision had fled—

*   *   *   *   *   *

CHANSON.

I KNOW you love me now
    Before I disbelieved,
And I will tell you how
    This fancy I conceived.

You thought me dead—and fear
    Prevented grief to speak :
Only a pearly tear
    Fell down your pallid cheek.

PARDONED.

JUDGES of Venice, wisest of men,
Grave and stern sat the Council of Ten :
    Who could their terrible thoughts surmise ?
Who could decipher their inner ken ;
    Black as the masks that screened their eyes.

Bring in the culprit the Council cried !
He who so daring our power defied :
    Loosen his fetters, slacken his chains
And should he lie to us, woe betide
    The prick of our wrath is full of pains !

The victim stood 'fore their piercing gaze
He dared with boldness his eyes to raise:
　　He seemed not to fear the brutes in black
And he shrank not from the scorching blaze
　　Of the fire that burned beside the rack.

He sought no mercy, he formed no plea,
He trembled not and his speech was free.
　　While the baffled Council scowled and frowned
By the laws of justice forced to see
　　That no proofs of treason could be found.

Well spoken hireling, now get thee hence
The Council pardons thy slight offence,
　　But e'er thou hiest, embrace yon shrine
For from the virgin a recompense
　　Thou well hast earned of her hand divine.

The victim hastened with joyous pace
And neared a statue, where, mild with grace
　　The blest Madonna stood carved in stone
With her arms outstretched, and saintly face,
　　Seeming to pity him from her throne.

Her sacred form he had scarce caressed
When he felt his body firmly pressed—
　　Two horrid arms with sharp daggers sprent
Nailed him inert to a knife-tipped breast
　　Till crushed and bleeding his limbs were rent.

　　*　　*　　*　　*　　*　　*　　*　　*

The statue swerves and the corse is thrown
From its fiendish clutch and grip of stone
　　Deep, deep in a hideous trap below
Where grim with their rippling monotone
　　Thick crimson waters ebb and flow.

Judges of Venice, wisest of men,
Grave and stern sat the Council of Ten :
　Who could their terrible thoughts surmise
Who could decipher their inner ken
　Black as the masks that screened their eyes.

BALLAD TO THE MOON.

　　Thou marvel of the night!
　　Flamant and argent eye,
　　　　Dizzy bright—
　　Why roamest thou so high?

　　My mind can ne'er unreave
　　The wonders of thy stare,
　　　　When each eve—
　　Beameth thy nitid glare.

　　Is it at times from grief
　　Thou mask'st thyself in clouds?
　　　　And relief—
　　Seek'st in their dusky shrouds?

　　Hast thou perchance a soul
　　Beneath thy blonden face
　　　　That can troul—
　　With thee through spheres of space?

　　Huge opal, set with stars!
　　The diamonds of the sky
　　　　Nothing mars—
　　The beauty of thine eye.

Canst thou not splendent orb
To queme a mystic mirth
　　All-absorb—
The glance of men from Earth?

Does not thy lustre harm
Some victim's witchèd gaze
　　By the charm
Of grim and vicious rays?

I call thee not a boon,
I even doubt thy sign
　　For oh moon!—
Oft fatal is thy shine!

Thou shed'st thy silv'ry sheen
Through lucid seas of blue—
　　Calm, serene,
But is that shimmering true?

I know not, but pretend
That thou dost take delight
　　To befriend—
All lovers when in plight.

When from a cloudy veil
Free, darts thy pallid leer
　　Softly pale—
Its fulgor stilleth fear.

Some beauty blushes deep,
Too far perhaps has strayed
　　Canst thou keep—
The secret of that maid?

For oft inopportune
Thou followest the pair,
    Curious moon—
Thou hast no business there!

I sometimes fear thy grin
Teems, though 'tis bland, of guile,
    And of sin—
Is carved thy crescent smile.

And more than that I think
When fleering on the snow,
    That thy blink—
Is dire for us below!

Its glisten on the rime,
Warns me with phantom tort
    That my time—
On Earth to live is short.

I sit with laden heart
Our gazes meet alway,
    What thou art—
My ken can never say.

Perhaps a fiend unhelled—
Punished by Gods to float
    And compelled—
Down on our world to gloat.

Forced to traverse the spheres,
And for man's welfare work
    For all years—
Though thy heart-hatreds lurk.

If true, how thou must burn
Dim with a thwarted rage,
    And must turn—
Vexed in thine azure cage!

Thy pearl-peep oft is sad,
Blank sad, as if in pain—
    And as mad,
Fleers thine oaf-eye again.

As lurid fulvous gold
Glow'st thou when autumn flies
    Icy cold—
Cloud-dappled in the skies.

Why does that other tinge
Of lush deep crimson lower?
    Dost thou cringe—
Beneath a rod of power?

I love thee o'er a lake
When thy gair rays immersed,
    Seem to slake—
A fierce and shining thirst.

And love thee when thy gleen
In fantasies of glow,
    Chilly keen—
Whitens the very snow!

I love to see thee shine
Over the castled gloom—
    On the Rhine:
When listed shadows loom.

The glaucous wavelets ebb,
Foam-woven by thy sheen
    In a web—
Of fire-pearls, white and green.

While as the hamlet prays,
Gambol on gabled roofs
    Airy fays—
Odd manikins and ouphs.

The eye-bloodshotten gnomes
Sport, whilst a siren chants
    As she combs—
Her hair from river plants.

The owl alone can brook
Thy frown when soaring by,
    And can look—
Up in thy globous eye.

Of thee a priceless boon
I ask when I am dead,
    And oh moon
Recall thee I have pled.

The power to grant is thine
For all from thee I crave,
    Is to shine—
Sadly upon my grave.

*   *   *   *   *   *

Huge opal set with stars
The diamonds of the sky,
    Nothing mars—
The beauty of thine eye.

CHINOISERIE.

EVERY steeple
Of Nankin did gleen and gleam,
When the people
Escorted with shout and scream,
* To the river's side—
My young Amoy bride—
Where a chû-built bark launched out in the stream
This maiden as fair as a silvery dream—

On the yellow
Light ochre-waved Yang-tse-Kiang,
To the mellow
Sonorous deep cling and clang,
Of gongs and of bells—
Resounding through dells—
In our guaïacum junk we glided and sang
Till the river reëchoed, reëchoed and rang.

Hard beladen
Our junk carried tea and tile,
And the maiden
Fair Hwâ of the "Amber smile,"
Who mused as she fanned—
Her cheek with small hand—
And gazed without trace of distrust or guile,
As we sailed on gaily for many a mile.

On we scudded
Through China to far Soutchou,
Lit and flooded
By skies of a turquoise blue,
While Hwâ chewed betel
Sipped tea, and would tell
Of her joy and her wonder at every new view
As we passed mangrove thickets and towns of bamboo.

And the splendor
Of midnight moons shed its glare,
On the tender
Hwâ, slender, frail young and fair,
As I kissed her feet—
So cunning and neat—
Half hidden by babouches, garnished rare
With pearls and with jazels, with beads and vair.

But a galley—
Of pirates, a heartless gang,
By a valley—
Concealèd, now on us sprang,
We in irons were bound—
But poor Hwâ was drowned—
Far out in the ochre-waved Yang-ste-Kiang
While the river with shrieks reëchoed and rang. . .

16*

MAD.

THE sun goes down—
The Heavens frown—
Far from the town—
   Why am I here ?
See the clouds swarm !
Each hath a form,
Can I keep warm ?
   Where shall I veer?

Bless thee oh rain !
Deluge the plain,
For I would fain—
   Quench my hot thirst.
Moan on and sigh,
Winds coursing by,
Mute will I lie,
   Mute and accursed . . .

What a dark night—
Shadows of fright
Menacing sight
   Dart by my side !
Will there no moon
Later or soon,
Shine opportune
   My steps to guide ?

Where can I find
I, sorrow-blind,
Somebody kind
  Light and a home?
Long have I strayed,
Who will bring aid
Why was I made
  Houseless to roam?

Would could I sleep,
Dance, shout or leap,
I cannot weep
  But I can *think*.
And I discern,
O'er fields of fern,
Big eyes that burn
  Big eyes that wink.

God! I am cold,
Blind, sick and old,
Yet I am bold—
  And I defy.
Snow and snow-flakes,
Ice and ice-lakes,
Serpents and snakes
  Hell, Earth and Sky.

For, does *she* know
I wander so
Cares she or no
  If I despair?

Peuh! she cannot
Pity my lot—
Much better rot,
   I do not care.

May she in Hell
Linger and dwell,
Until the smell
   Of her scorcht flesh—
Sicken the flames,
And may her shames
Sins and bad aims
   Crackle afresh.

Oh how my brain
Trembles with pain:
Phantoms insane
   Hoot for my death.
Air, wood, all things
Vanish on wings.
Hotter than stings
   Burneth my breath.

Were I a child,
Pure, undefiled,
Pleasure beguiled
   Were I a boy—
From the tree-tops,
Rain that ne'er stops,
All the hot drops,
   I would enjoy.

But I am worn
Drenched, and grief-torn
Longing for morn
   So I will creep—
Here by this tomb,
'Neath the oak's gloom
I will find room,
   To die . . . or sleep . . .

TO A COQUETTE.

THY beauty stirs a subtle pain
   I breathe with thine own perfumed air,
As, speechless, mad of heart and brain
   I fail to check my amorous care :
Though wishing it were stilled and slain.
   Should I rebel, or should I dare
To crave thy kisses' unctuous rain
   With heartfelt sigh, or truest prayer,
I feel thy laughing voice would wane . . . .
   I know thy wondering glances, gair
Would mark me like a scar or stain,
   I could not brook their torturing stare.
And I would be a brute profane
   Should I by flattery strive to tear—
One lustrous look from thee : oh deign
   My racked and suffering sense to spare,
Tell me but once that thou wouldst fain
   With kisses fond, with titles fair

Destroy the mordant, jealous bane
　　My heart can find no strength to bear !
For why should my proud wish, inane
　　If so it be, not win and share
The bliss of love with thee, and gain
　　Those carnal joys, so rich and rare ?
But no, thou let'st me plead in vain
　　Thou gaily mockest my despair,
But dost thou think I will remain
　　Ever as true as I declare ?
Coquette take heed, use less disdain
　　Coquette take heed, think well, beware !

LINES TO A CORPSE.

MUTE pallid mass of withering flesh inert,
　　Thou know'st the secret that I fain would learn.
　　Thy useless carcass doth no longer burn
With thy flown soul's rich vivid warmth: alert
It soars in spheres unknown, unchecked, unhurt,
　　The sweets of which the body cannot earn.
If that soul can perceive, which I assert
　　How must it loathe thy ugliness, and spurn
Thy purple putrid swollen breast of dirt,
Wherein each avid worm awaits its turn . . . .

Yea ! till it sickens, with hot tears of pain
　　It hovers o'er thy shrouds with jealous care
　　It lingers in thy coffin's cryptish air
Although to seek a purer realm 'twould fain.

It waits on noiseless wings till thou hast lain
   In rotting rest for months, till gaunt and bare
Thy decomposing bones have cloyed the drain
   Of Earth's absorbing, till thy vital share
By occult changes serves the world again
   Till mildew, rust and muck once more are fair.

Then when some full-blown rose in after days
   Upon thy tombstone's mound brings forth its red—
   Rich beauty : which by thy foul carrion fed,
Bloomed from its essence in mysterious ways
Up to the genial warmth of sunnier rays.
   Thy weary wandering soul forgets its dread,
And to the Maker chaunting spirit lays,
   Infuses love upon thy fragrant head
Mingles itself and blends with thee—and prays
   To One who brings to life what once was dead.

SONNET.

DEEP in the claustral glooms of pillared aisles
   I wandered to tempt calm : Toledo slept.
Its grand cathedral, lit by pearl-pale smiles—
   From stars,—mused with the night, while o'er it
      crept—
Grey waves of shadows, as I hushed my guiles
   And, at the virgin's altar knelt, and wept ;—
Wept o'er my deep wild thoughts, o'er wishful wiles,
   O'er sins that mocked my strength, o'er sins .that
      slept . . . .

For hours strove I to still the brutal yearn
That urged me to betray thy youth, and spurn
Thy love immaculate for fleshy pain,
    But even at the shrine of martyred Christ
The flowers of vice within me bloomed again,
    Hell was my God—and Hell thy soul enticed. . . .

MOSAIC.

I HAVE seen in my magical dreams,—
    Of colorful days and of nights;
A ravishing vista of gleams,
    Of glamours, of reds, and of whites.

A landscape in Aidens unknown,
    A scene to bewilder the eye:
Where a sun of fire topazes shone—
    Through a glimmering sapphire sky.

In those luminous realms of space,
    Clouds of opal soared suavely by,
And reflected their smiling grace,
    In a sea of turquoise dye.

On an agate and jasper shore
    The waves darted pearls in spray,
And the melody of their roar
    Swelled in gems of iris ray.

Lofty mountains of malachite
  Rose beyond all crowned in mist,
Clear, diaphanous, gair and bright,
  Like a molten amethyst!

And their violet tips illumed
  A forest of emerald leaves,
Where small ruby flowers perfumed
  The twilights of dazzling eves.

On the porphyry branches sung
  Wee birds with a grace untold,
Diamond-eyed and with garnet tongue,
  With feathers of burnished gold!

And each atom was diadem,
  And when night upon all set
The moon like a giant gem,
  Shone white through a sea of jet!

And banks of coral I saw,
  And amber and lapis and pearls,
And crystal lakes virgin of flaw
  That revelled in scintillant whirls.

When the sun was declining, its hue
  With the golds and the greens would blend,
And the fusing of all with blue,
  Seemed like rainbows without end!

But amidst all these marvels of worth,
  In this world of precious stone,
There was naught to recall our Earth
  But one thing and that alone—

On an emerald twig o'erhead
  Perched a beautiful snow-white dove,
'Twas the soul of Marie now dead,
  Marie whom I used to love !

CHARLES BAUDELAIRE.

GIANT of fancies grand, sun-perfumed soul !
  Thy bubbling thoughts held revel in thy brain;
  Thy songs of sorrows sad, mistrusts and pain
In rhythmic harmonies forever roll.
Thy spirit-muse sought out the vivid *whole*
  Of vast conceits : it spurned all tare, while grain,
  Sweet grain, of wondrous sweetness by it lain
Proves that thy soaring soul attained its goal.
  Thou king of voyellous words, of puissant rhyme,
  Thy clear eye saw beyond all Night, all Time,
Yet have thy regal musings left no trace.
  Dead, thou art still ignored—no welcome nod
Acclaims thy ghost ; few knew thy name or face
  Thou of all poets who could speak with God !

THE YUNGFRAU.

Magnet of ice ! white-eyed, supreme, immense !
　　Thy grand imperial whitenesses of awe—
　　Blur all my songful thought, and potent, draw—
Into thy bosom's glooms my wandering sense ;
Rapt by the sheen diaphanous, intense
　　Of thy white virgin beauty, free of flaw.
　　Thy stiff cold tears of sdain that never thaw
All promise death as choicest recompense
To me, if I but cling to thee and climb
Thy giant breasts of frosts, thy flanks of rime,
Or scale thy treacherous steeps to topmost peaks
　　And brave thy avalanche's dreaded flow !
Then shall I find what all my body seeks,
　　A tomb sublime in seas of endless snow !

AN ANSWER.

A studio—a smouldering fire—shelves of books—dead light—a table covered with volumes, manuscripts, chemical instruments, etc.

A STUDENT.

OH wondrous mysteries of Art and Lore,
    I shrink beneath your mightiness, in pain—
Of mental sweets: while all I still ignore
    Vast worlds of subtle thought that flee my brain,
Deride with virgin stubbornness, a soul—
    O'erflusht with science: while a frenzied ken
Chafes to attain a thinker's cherished goal,
    And learn all things unknown to other men. . .

I strive and toil in vain, eye-worn and sick—
    Of shadowy prose veiling an occult theme.
I long to feel a genial blood flow thick—
    Through all my thought-cowed body, in a stream
Of roused and virile joyfulness, to purge
    A torpid maze of thinkings: but alas!
I lack a will such buoyancy to urge,
    Much had I better count the hours that pass.

An arid pleasure find I, when the sound—
    Nervous, recurrent, of my clock I hear.
When link by link, the chain of hours unwound
    Clings with its rhythmèd sameness on my ear.

192

The solemn warner oft unthanked, relieves—
  Oppressing silence ; harbinger of woe,
And cheers a mind, which anguish-stricken grieves,
  Boiling to speed its never hast'ning flow—

What in huge dusty volumes have I learnt
  To draw the color to my palsied cheek ?
To ease my aches of heart, cark-stifled, burnt
  By furious gloat for fame ; by musings weak ?
What in the vaguenesses of Copt or Zend
  Have I solved, that unriddled could beguile
Or please my fancy, when the brutal end
  Brought but the pleasure of a sceptic smile ?
" Nebulous secrets of old Arab skill,
  Runes of the Northern clime so oddly formed,
Maxims and legend-flowers culled from Motril,
  When on the Spanish coast the Moslem swarmed—
Marvels and glories of the Eastern lands,
  Tales of chill Ukraine's steppes in mystic sense,
Echoes of Khiva's turrets, Egypt's sands,
  Have ye e'er caused me such a joy immense—
As when I watched the blonden moonbeams play
  In lustrous streams of light upon the sea,
Blending their argent shadows with the spray
  Cresting the rugged cliffs in watery glee" ? . .
But now e'en that joy sickens : Nature's charms
  Cannot allure by planets or by flowers,
Withered by all the world's deceitful harms,
  Spurn I a faith in God's assuaging powers.
Stolid and worn, in studies rapt, I dreamt—
  A surcease of pale chagrin I could find—
But fashioned wiser, view I with contempt
  The verbose fodder crunched to feast my mind.

AN ANGEL.

Nay, youngling, say not so, for time
  Has-proven clement : and thy years
Count not as yet a mortal's prime.
  Why shouldst thou tire of life, that cheers—
When ably tasted : and when spent
  In noble toilings as thou hast—
Nursing repose and calm content
  Surely thy joys are joys that last !

STUDENT.

'Tis false, they queme me not—my brain afire,
Is goaded by their temptings to aspire—
To spheres of thought above :—beyond my reach,
Which no dry tome or parchment can e'er teach.
My rhapsodies are boundless, and my flight—
Of fancies soars through chaos and through night,
Until my will, too frail, pain-checked, is crushed,
By powers unknown, and all its fevers hushed. . .

ANGEL.

Student, art rash ! and shouldst not strive
Thy feeble ponderings to drive—
Beyond the limits drawn for man
By sapient hands on Earth to span.
Rest thee awhile : or else in Love. . . .
Mayst find the key to bliss above.

STUDENT.

Speak not of Love, fair vision, I implore.
I dreamt its pangs I felt—but now ignore
Its every meaning :—though that myth I blessed
When, vain, elated loon, I first caressed
A demon, seraph-faced, of maddening form,
Whose hot, wet, Hell-drugged kisses, lava-warm,
With am'rous velvet touchings, to my core—
Stung; with such joy-lost fervor, that if more
And more of this soul-wavering delight
She had refused, I would by passion's might
Have strangled out caresses from her breath—
And would have burnt them kiss-scorcht into Death.
Why did I not—a budding love I gave
To her already tainted grip :—a slave—
To her one, every wish was I; but when,
In webbèd ardors welded fiercely, then—
The traitrous siren loved me—*I* was all,
Her God and Universe—and she the thrall !
And yet, with elfen subtlety, this maid
My love of loves with infamy betrayed.
I could not kill her—for my dirk atilt,
Sank in her gallant's weasand to the hilt :
And ere the reeking blade I had withdrawn
To spill her lying blood—the wench had gone !
But now my heart is ironed and free of grief,
And that is why I sneer at Love's belief !

ANGEL.

Thou shouldst have pardoned since, when time and
    years
Have stilled the torrent of thy jaundiced tears.
What whim unslaked, gnaweth thy nettled breast,
That stayeth heart's repose, that checketh rest?
If love is quenched the envious tide runs deep.
What are thy evil aims at night, when sleep—
By febrile recollections baulked, has lost
Its soothing power—when, on thy pillow tossed,
The hours seem ages, and the slumber sought
Unnerves and deadens every wish peace-fraught?
Can it be hate that grimes thy sleepless eves
With foul-mouthed yearn, and does the web it weaves
Of honeyed promise, ravel in thy mind
A knot of vengeance arduous to unwind?

STUDENT.

No, no, fair vision, my erst hates have flown,
My ires by toils have dumb and callous grown:
Hate is a useless passion, twin to crime
So deem I—but when young it is sublime
To hate, while every fibre thrills a frame
Rabid with haughty rage—alas, too tame
And vimless now! its sting can never vex
A soul impassible to life's sad wrecks.
For, if its virus foul could drop by drop,
Ooze in my heart, my poisoned thought would stop—
And counteract its bitterness by gall,
That direr venom, servant to my call!

ANGEL.

Thy speech is odious, and thy rattling tongue
Prateth 'gainst reason ; but I know thee young—
And not devoid of feeling, thou canst yet
All woman's wrongs to thee, and men's forget.
Thy heart is warm, beneath an algid pride,
Its olden flame will flicker, and a guide—
In me wilt find ; whose counsel will uphold
And strengthen debile faith—hope-guarded, bold,
Thou shouldst essay a glorious end to claim,
For with thy innate genius, wealth and fame,
Those all-prized treasures will thy trophies be,
And such a lot, depends . . .

STUDENT.

On whom ?—

ANGEL.

—On thee.

STUDENT.

Cherub, thy cautioning cannot avail,
I come of no foul, rotten stock, to wail—
And sorrow for ambition's sweet, or pine
To hear the world's opinion on a line
Or phrasing that I pen, for I prefer
To sip my life-cup's mingled wine and myrrh,
In silence, and from all the world conceal,
The passions and emotions that I feel.

Call'st thou ambitious one who greeds to rule
A horde of savage soldiers armed in steel,
Who straggle to the fray as would a mule
Kicked at and battered by his master's heel?
Deem'st thou ambitious he whose subjects bleed
And perish by his orders, on a field
Where belching cannon, deaf to race or creed,
Vomit their terrors till the foemen yield?
Deem'st thou ambitious one in pomp arrayed
With slaves and cohorts at his erst command,
One who is wealthy-pursed and strong of blade,
One whose omnipotence awes sea and land?
If so, he lacketh reason, less his life
Be one of leniency; for tyrants' sleep
Is sad and fatal, and a rancorous knife
Can sound the infamy of hearts most deep.

ANGEL.

Thy soul is gelid to emotion, and
Thy doggèd will, by listlessness unmanned,
Spurns that which other men would die to gain.
Surely art born of flesh, thou dreadest pain,
Thou hast a love, a hate, a pride or fear,
Some woful loss has blighted thy career.
Has lack of care and fondness made thee mad?

STUDENT.

No dearth of true affection have I had—
A hidden grief perchance, but that will dwell
Within my vitals, till the heats of Hell—
Burn and consume it out, when nerve and blood
Are dried and scorchèd by the fiery flood.

A Phantom.

Valiantly spoken, youth—I know thy need.
Thou gloar'st for gold—thy fantasy to lead
In paths of luxury, for hadst thou power
A fortune and a palace at this hour
Would clothe thy limbs, and would thy head protect,
While happy, young and reckless, wouldst elect,
And choose thy mistresses, thy friends and slaves,
Rich regal days, is what thy notion craves—

Student.

Spirit, thou liest—naught of gold I ask—
I am no wizard with a baffling mask
Screening a secret in each blear dull eye,
All I demand is, as the days roll by—
Leaving me tranquil in my bitter gloom
To muse on thoughts oft-weighed, of after tomb.
Gold to my nature serveth not—its chink
Sounds dead upon my ear—and when I think
How other fools adore it—then I laugh,
And titter cynic o'er the wine I quaff.
What can I need of gold? To win a friend?
A man who follows me, until I spend
The last cursed farthing, and who will declare
That although generous I was hard to bear,
Full of strange whims, proud, spiteful and perverse,
Simply 'cause he had naught and I the purse?
Nay, nay, no metal can e'er buy the scene
I built in dreams—a landscape autumn-green,
High lofty mountains, tipped with nitid snow
Tinted by purple heavens—and, below,

A cot, white, simple, hidden by a ring
Of firs and poplars, where the wood-larks sing
And purl their joyful hymns when sunbeams stream
Upon the rustling foliage :—that my dream
Has been, but now, has faded—chased by cark,
Leaving me Life, abhorrent—blank and dark.

CHORUS OF ANGELS.

On banks of flowers,
The summer hours
   Invite sweet sleep.
In dreams of charm—
Thy soul from harm—
And evil powers,
   Our wings will keep.

STUDENT.

I need no sleep !

CHORUS OF DEMONS.

On lakes of fire,
In regions dire
   With us wilt roam ?
In seas of flame—
Thy soul can claim—
   Its mute desire,
With sylph and gnome.

STUDENT.

I need no home !

PHANTOM.

I wis thy greed, a riot, hot embrace
From lips of rose—a lust-paled, upturned face
With luring eyes, thine eyes' strong glance to pierce,
Tempests of sighs to quell in torpors fierce.
A silken forest of blonde curls to toss
And tangle round thy fingers, till its gloss—
Gair, yellow and exciting, tempt thy whim
In prurient ecstasies to plunge and swim,
As when the sea-gull, cresting o'er the wave
Dotes on its bosom's foam, wherein to lave
Its fruitless passion, while its plaintive shriek
Implores a fickle love till wings are weak.

STUDENT.

Spirit a parnel's hug I cherish not
A strumpet markets out her body's rot
And plays her foulest comedy to prove
An absent passion : can such mockery move
A man to hanker for her venomed press,
And pay with gold, the gall of her caress ?
Think'st thou for such pale drazels I would leave
My fire and room, and lecherous I would grieve
And blubber like a stripling for a whore
The trifle of a hundred rakes before ?

CHORUS OF ANGELS.

The sunbeams spread
Their fulgor red
On grove and wood :

All Nature sings
Of God all things
Below, o'erhead,
　Are fair and good.

Chorus of Demons.

The twilight falls,
Our Master calls,
　His voice through night
Resoundeth shrill,
Art stubborn still,
What fear appals?
　O! haste thy flight.

Student.

What I loved most was Color, for my eye
By varied tints and hues of Nature's dye
Grew ravished:　When the blinding sky-blue pours
Its sheen immaculate on reed-clad shores,
The lucid water toucht with fulvid streams
Of golden splendor, sun-kisst, glows and gleams.
Each bubbling ripple, white as lady's hand
Dashes, pearled, plastic on the hot red sand
Of some broad beach, with shells and alga sprent
Green, brown, blue, yellow, strangely blent!
And oh! what velvet tints the elm-tree's bark
Rugose and gnarry, taketh, when the spark
Of fire-flies' nacarat twinkling lumes the trunk
When on huge curving boughs, the linnets, drunk—
With gracious melody, chirp, purl and trill
From downy throatlets, till their voices fill

The silent wood, while bird and leaf and rush
Await that sacred hour, when, white of flush
The prying moon—mist-dotted, vapor-ploughed,
Escapes from 'neath its drapery of cloud,
And deluges the forest in its grace :
While, slumb'ring near, the artist's placid face
Pale, by moon paler, dreams and loves and lives
By Color's power, and all the bliss it gives—

ANGEL.

In all thy roamings hast thou had no gust,
No like or no distemper, taste or trust?
Hast thou in God's grand temples prayed or knelt,
Hast thou e'er piety within thee felt?
When, in the Mosque or Kirk the rites began
When quivering voices begged that sins of man
Would lessen—? did no inner chord awake
Proud and triumphant, noble? didst not make
Some resolution, didst thy doubt repent
Its sluggishness, didst clamor to give vent
In virile action to thy backward life . . . ?

STUDENT.

No thought as this was in my bosom rife.
All I enjoyed with ravish, was the grace
Of Titian's glowing virgins, and their face
One, only face all-holy, filled my heart
With sweets seraphic, and would ease the smart—
Of terrene unbelief :—as long I gazed
Upon his glorious painting, color-crazed.
But then I thought I loved him, and no love—
On Earth, or Hell below, and Heaven above

Rivals the contemplation of the Art
Of Italy's great masters :—why depart
From such care-calming worship?—who can paint
Christ livid, crucified, with halo faint
Around a thorn-crowned brow like Reni's hand,
What is more vivid, truthful, pious, grand—
Of horror? and of colors blent—the sponge
Seems sour and swollen: see ! the soldiers lunge
Their barbèd spears deep in the withered flesh
Do not lorn Mary's tears fall all afresh?
Murillo, angel-haunted, wields the gift
Visions of grace from heavenly clouds to lift.
His mild Madonna glance, true, pure and bright
Equals the stars' in brilliancy of light—
Only a light of glory, made to bless
A light of mercy no pale orbs possess . . . .
Rubens, of florid touch becharmed me oft,
His wealthy-bosomed sirens, sinewed soft
Denoting strength and suppleness combined,
Have magnetized my willing eye and mind.
Van Dyck, with tints of gloom, has fashioned forms
Alluring by their verity ; while swarms
Of chimeras, and visions, quaintly odd
Besiege the memory, while dark portraits nod
Their wrinkled heads, closed in the massive frame
And wink triumphant on the signer's name.
Rembrandt, sad shadows, altars and a pyx !
The horrent splendors of the crucifix !
Portraits, and heads, bald, bearded—joy and woe
Toucht with a glow of winter's rime and snow.
Watteau ! light, fickle airy whims of oil
A ball's coquette, a revelry's turmoil

Silk, satin, ribbons, flowers and powdered hair
A court, a garden, moonbeams here and there;
Wigged, sworded courtiers, held 'twixt love and fight
The whole depicted, half in pink, half white!
Steen, with his simple brush has quemed me vast,
When, gay of mind, I sought to rouse the past
Of Holland's dorps, and view his village scenes:
A burgomeister on a table leans—
Within a cabin clean as falling flakes.
A kitten by the fire its naplet takes—
Upon the floor, plump peach-cheeked children play
Near by, the buxom housewife knits away
While, o'er a pewter tankard, cool with beer
The father smiles upon the ones so dear . . .
Ah pass! that paint brought tears: grim Goya's muse
Other far ghastlier dyes was wont to use.
Th' Escurial sombre in its stony vale,
Peopled within its crypt by spectres pale.
Blood-clotted pools—wan eyes and haggard looks,
Clouds grey as twilight—black-rimmed: rooks—
Gaunt ravens, shades of sorrow, rotting bones,
The shriek of maiden ravished, and the groans
Of tortured martyrs; marshes, fenny-dank
Hoidens with giggling jaws—the iron clank
Of gyves rust-eaten, bull-fights, gore and fire
Naught save the noxious, horrent, and the dire.
Fantastic Ribera would oft unhinge
The bolts of fear-barred thought—and tinge
His pallid corpses with that bluish touch
That fills th' expectant worm within with grutch:
His cult was ugliness: the master's hand
From horrors brought forth Beauty at command,

Beauty victorious in some bleeding Christ,
Beauty all potent in his Death unpriced !
Now, Color as my other loves, submerged—
In waves of listlessness, by mind-rods scourged,
Cannot e'en to a moment's joy give birth
I live indifferent to its charm and worth,
And no oil-dabbled picture chaste or lewd
Can tempt me back unto the muse I wooed . . .

ANGEL.

Pagan of hardened fancies : canst thou sneer
E'en at thy stage of unbelief, when ear
And soul are captured by some gentle strain
Of soothing melody ? hear'st thou again
Without a throb of feeling tunes that rocked
Thy infant form to slumber ? hast thou mocked
With senseless tongue the balm of Music's power,
That abstract love, by gods bequeathed as dower ?
Hath thy heart fluttered when the church-bell's chimes
Rang out their brazen wealth of holy rhymes ?
Has not the organ's mellow, measured voice,
Ever an accent found to please thy choice ?

STUDENT.

Angel, the tunes of olden time bring back
Hosts of harmonious sorrows—sad and black—
As envy : my imprisoned thoughts unbound
Once more, and free, drink up their well-known sound :
But then I sudden veer, and flee them fast
Cursing the tell-tale memories of the past.
The music of my simmering thoughts console
My wretchedness, and with my grief condole

A music vague and sombre—born of tears,
A music grave and sad :—a phantom leers
Over each chosen note, and terrifies
My soul quiescent as the Hell-sounds rise.
Weber alone—grim thinker—was inspired
From worlds most nebulous—for he admired
The strident moanings of the German night,
Seas of strange melody, so wild of fright
In all their magic rhythms, new and bold,
Teeming with weirdities of style untold.
He of all dreamers spoke in sob and wail
He of all dreamers tore the subtle veil
Off mystic beauty, and disrobed her form
Which nude was cold, but by his kissings warm
Grew docile and her secret wealth laid bare
To one who sought the music of the Air—
The leaflet's whirr, the valley-streamlet's notes,
Sad melodies from forests, or from throats
Of night-birds in the Schwarzenwald's deep shade
And who of all a mighty concert made—
Puissant of grace, wonder of sylphic sound
Sought for by ardor, and by ardor found.
I understood his vague mellifluous tongue,
My sceptic heart, his sceptic ditties sung,
But now all Music's sweets I shun and mock
And I prefer the music of my clock ! . . . .

ANGEL.

Thou who avowest life is hard to bear
Findest thou transport in the joy of prayer?

Ignorest thou the raptures of a soul
Invoking Gods whose mercies can console. . . . ?

STUDENT.

Angel, thou temptest me, my views are frail
And bottomless of things terrene : why fail
In mad essaying to decipher creeds
The mystic problem that solution needs
Of life beyond this life ?—can man assume
To solve the secrets of the after tomb ?
E'er to transfuse the soul that in him lives
E'er to define the breath his mother gives ?
Science is vast, and brains by thought consume,
But who can lift the veil of doubt and gloom
Screening the phantom future like a shroud,
Leaving all mortals baffled, foiled and cowed.
I cannot speak. . . . .

ANGEL.

Believest thou ?—

STUDENT.

—In what ?

ANGEL.

In powers supreme that fix and shift thy lot,
That either wound or kill, sustain, create,
That rule thy doings, and command thy fate ?

STUDENT.

Spirit ! a sacrilege thou mayst suspect
But hark thee ! all religions I respect

As good and worthy,—but believe in none.
The bronze-skinned savage who adores the sun,
And bows before the flamant eye in fear
Should not be scoffed at, if his voice sincere,
In simple wordings swelleth out in prayer
To one that warms and feeds him by its glare.
The Parsees kneeling to their God of Fire
Ascend with cheerful steps a blazing pyre
To perish faithful—girt with strong belief—
Do they not merit for their martyred grief
An envied life of joys in other spheres,
As consolation for their worldly fears?
Cannot a noble heart in Greek or Turk
In breast of Jew, as well as Christian lurk?
The struts and splendors of the Orient's rites
The pageants, jewelled costumes, countless lights,
The wailing dervishes with sandalled feet,
The censers swinging with their perfumes sweet,
The sumptuous mosques, marvels of Eastern art
The tekkès domed, chiselled in every part
With crafty hand, till stone resembles lace,
A glorious tribute, age cannot efface—
The sensuous music, velvet to the ear,
Monotonous of rhythm, sad, austere,
Yet soul vibrating, mystic, gravely sung,
By throat melodious, and by fervent tongue:
The stately Imans robed in white and blue,
The zaims, defenders, eunuchs, retinue,
Steel, gold and glory, pomp immense,
Does not this speak to eye, to soul, to sense,
Persuading all as loud the muezzin drones,
"Allah is great, Mahomet's love atones,"

Should Moslem faith be jeered at, flouted, cursed,
If not the best of creeds, is it the worst?
Am I to mock the rites of Manitou,
The power of Siva, Brahma or Vischnu?
The stellèd vales of Delhi and Lahore
Still celebrate their mercies as of yore.
Why should we modern unbelievers grin,
And chuckle o'er a rite we call a sin?
Quetzalcoàtl's priests and slaves adored
A brutal god of serpents, grimed, begored,
While Norseland's brawny warriors sought the fray
And corse-strewn fjelds, to prove great Odin's sway
Blood—crime and slaughter, be it, but they fought
And slew with faith—a faith that should be taught
To our poor shallow-minded priests, who tell
In verbose sermons that the pains of Hell
All sinners shall endure, whilst Hell on Earth
Exists as well as Paradise from birth—
Their faith is blind and tottering, bought by gold
Unwarmed by Nature's charms—their prattle cold
And nine of ten would use their Saviour's curse
To draw a farthing in their greedy purse. . . .
The faith of chivalry, the art of Moor
Will to my fancy greater joys procure
Than any creed, discussed by changing whim.
Religions' depths are nebulous and dim,
And if I had belief—which I have not
Shunning all crumbling ages' rust and rot,
I would my trust place in the world of art
Speaking to soul, to spirit, sense and heart.

What faith was nobler than the faith of gold
That spurred the ancient architects, untold—
Unbidden, save by Art's great voice, to toil
And spread their genius-seed on native soil?
Mammoth cathedrals built they, aisled and naved
Columns on columns, chiselled, wrought, engraved
Poems of granite, symphonies of stone !
Silent yet soulful, mighty, in the lone—
Vague twilight of the ages—as they seem
To stretch their steeples to a God supreme
Like two huge giant hands imploring grace
Far in the deep blue densities of space—
Chartres, Antwerp, Rheims, of art the choicest flower
Seville's Giralda, with its rosy tower,
Toledo, Burgos of the sculptured dome—
Cordova—Beauvais, Strasbourg, Sens, and Rome
Moscow's St. Basil with its zebraed heights
Upsala's grandeur, where the gloom delights—
A pensive muse—all gems of patient skill   .
Erected by a few great men, whose will
Was strong as tempests, and their faith as strong :
For well knew they the painful work, and long
They planned, and that a century would pass
Before a form symmetric graced the mass.
The bliss of witnessing their task fulfilled
Was not their lot—they knew it—yet unstilled
Were Faith and Ardor—while the day they died
The lofty temple grew in strength and pride—
Oh ! that is faith in art ! and yet the name
Of those heroic strugglers—lost to fame
Is now ignored, save by some monk austere,
Who reads the church's archives once a year
And who perchance may treasure in his mind,
The name of one who labored for mankind.

PHANTOM.

Art strangely novel, for thou hast no quest
No wish, no covet—dream'st thou not at best
Of some fair vision, modelled in thy mind
Of gnomish beauty—fulvid eyed, to blind
Thy gaze by rapturous blinkings, green of tint,
Chasms of smaragd lust—of boiling glint
What need'st thou?

STUDENT.

Naught.

ANGEL.

What need'st thou?

STUDENT.

Naught, I say—
The roseate clouds of dawn announce the day;
Spirits of Good and Evil, here I swear
That naught of happiness, and naught of care
Can stir my lethargy; my fibres mute
Love sleep alone, and food, as would a brute;
For having lived and seen, my soul is sore,
Mortals may call me mad, and vile of core
But all I wish—

ANGEL.

Well speak poor heart of stone!

STUDENT.

All that I wish is to be left alone ! . . . . . .

THE FIR.

On autumn nights I love to err
    Far in the Forest's depths: beneath—
The sombre foliage of the fir,
    Shading the verdure of the heath.

I love to ponder in the gloom
    And hear the breezes rustle by:
Breathing their wafts of sweet perfume
    Scenting the starry domes of sky.

Long russet leaves all dry and sere
    Crackle beneath my idle tread,
The crisp soft sound delights my ear
    The sound of tears the firs have shed !

The knarry oak, the slender pine,
    The frowning cedar's ghastly shade—
All lend a subtle charm divine
    My dreamy senses to pervade.

Each dew-steeped flow'ret seems to smile
    Revealing scented worlds of bliss
In each pied chalice's profile,
    When quivering 'neath the rush's kiss.

The nimble squirrel spooms in fear
  Before my steps with plaintive moan,
The thrushes' trilling voices near
  Blend with the lively cricket's drone.

I love the vast and mighty scene
  I love the fire-fly's mystic light.
Piercing with twinkling smaragdine—
  The opaque shroud of ombrèd night.

But, when the moonbeam's lustre blonde
  Streams down in lambent tides of glare,
My pulsing heart-chords soft respond
  My eyes gloar wildly in the air.

Gauze-clad and sylphic, 'fore my gaze
  Sweet chimera of youth and grace,—
Floats like a milky opal's blaze
  An airy form with pallid face.

Face ! form ! like Dolci's virgins : save—
  The silv'ry whiteness of the breast
Where spherèd twins seem e'er to crave
  The dainties of a riot rest.

I by this dazzling sight revive
  And burn to murmur all my love,
I cannot stir . . . . in vain I strive—
  The phantom frail still soars above.

Caressing spirals of soft light
  Emerge ; at ev'ry flamant gyre
The cruel dryad draws through night,
  My witchèd passion to inspire.

The nacreous spirit fades away
   Encircled by the moonlet's beam
*   *   *   *   *   *   *   *
Black night dawn-mingled, shuns the day
   I wake: the vision is a dream !

And that is why I love to err
   Far in the Forest's depths: beneath
The sombre foliage of the fir
   Shading the verdure of the heath—

And that is why when I am dead
   I wish to slumber in a tomb,
Where fir-leaves rustle o'er my head,
   Where at my feet wild daisies bloom.

THE SUCCUBE.

THOU Succube with opal eyes dreaming,
   Thou ghoul of a ravishing form;
Thou siren with mysteries teeming,
   Thy kissings were splendid and warm !
The glare of thine eyes and their gleaming—
   Caused passions to hover and swarm.

Thou wert lavish oh temptress of kisses,
   Of kisses far sweeter than wine;
There was Death in our joys and our blisses,
   With a shroud didst my love-life entwine,
And thy hot tongue hell-cloven of hisses,
   Pierced a heart that was mine and was thine.

'Neath the sting of thy love have I cowered
    A love that breathed death at each sigh:
Broken, wearied, I prayed thee, o'erpowered,
    To avert thy black luminous eye—
The caresses thy burning lips showered
    Were false, yet I knew not their guy!

Thou wert sanctioned by demons to kill me,
    To cloy me with sweetness and joys:
Thou wert bidden to glut and o'erfill me,
    With the sound of thy ravishing voice;
Thou wert ordered to chill me and thrill me
    With thy kissings' soft murmurous noise.

And I found that thy body was rotten,
    I found that thine eye hid no tear:
I learned that thy heart had forgotten,
    Every tie that was holy and dear;
I found that thy brain was begotten—
    In sin, and a sluttish career.

So I know thee and all my thought-arrows
    A target will make of thine heart:
I will send thee a cursing that harrows
    I will make thee more hellish than art!
And the sting of my hates in thy marrows,
    Will burn thee with splendors of smart!

DIALOGUE.

In gloomful crypts most tenebrous, below—
   The granite arching of a vaulted tomb,
Imbedded in the dark dead dirt, where flow—
   The dank cloacas of the earth's vast womb;
Down where no atom of pale light can glow,
   Where morbid miasms rise, of rank perfume,
Hewn of the tough and nodous larch-trees' wood
Two mammoth open coffins upright stood—

Within, two skeletons lay firmly prest—
   By rusty clasps of rugged iron in bands,
Two slime-gnawed skulls, perhaps by final quest
   Hung loosely swinging; while four bony hands
Were crossed and nailed upon each ghastly breast,
   Seeming to supplicate with vague demands—
While oozing from the stone arch of the crypt,
Great drops of foulest water soilward dripped.

Brother, said one, here have we rotted years
   Far from the sunlight of our soul and flesh.
Here have our corpses shed those gallful tears
   Of spite and thwarted hates, whose salts refresh.
I have been witness to thy speechless fears,
   I saw thy noiseless struggles in thy mesh—
Of iron and wood: and saw thy trembling head
Kissed by the worms, like mine, till they were fed.

Now art thou bone, so I, and peace at last
   Is left us for a period to enjoy.
Our hard stiff ribs resist—though time flies fast,
   No vermine can our skeletons destroy,
Till we have told our stories of the past !
   Then can yon grutching toads await their cloy,
For days must fade before our remnants rust,
For years must pass ere we again are dust.

Brother, the life I left, its light and sun,
   Its pains and pleasures I do not regret :
All things have end, all joys when erst begun
   Please and delight ;—they last not longly, yet—
Wise is the man who takes them one by one,
   Learning to prize their sweet, and time forget,
Live for his day, however short, and curse
A phantom future with a shroud and hearse.

Alas ! I did not, and my fleeting time
   Was spent in assays to acquire and learn
The mysteries of loreful prose and rhyme :
   Knowledge and science brought me no return.
Nights passed in toil, wanderings in ev'ry clime
   Comforted little :—while for more would yearn—
My thirsty brain, until this coffin's clasp
Taught me one secret which I ne'er could grasp

The plans and projects that I formed on earth,
   My endless strife to make a name and mark,
The thoughts and fancies which I deemed of worth,
   The constant stress upon my talent spark,

What have they proven? why their forcèd birth?
   Can they give light unto us dead and dark;
Can fame bring succor to this den of dirt,
Can my poor bones their freedom now assert?

My science can avail me not, and gold,
   Great piles of bright new gold I used to prize,
Cannot relieve our withering frames from cold
   Nor fill the void of dull and vanished eyes:
And yet I loved my opulence untold,
   My soul was poisoned by the metal's ties;
I kept it, with it did no mortal good:—
The same who took it made my coffin's wood!

So had I choice again I would not care
   To taste of life a second bitter draught;
If it were given to me unaware—
   It might be sourer than the one I quaffed—
Earth air is fresh, while here the fetid air—
   Poisons the grumous vermine at each waft,
Yet I prefer this sombre, solemn life
To one above of ceaseless cark and strife.

Brother, the listening skeleton replied,
   'Thy useless life was not like mine but sad:
I owned no gold, nor loved I lore, defied—
   All laws, religions, creeds both good and bad,
I lived for pleasure, and by pleasure died,
   A better life than thine, more glad, more mad
A life of revelries, of song, and mirth;
A life of thirty years thy sixty's worth!

Mocking eternity, deriding pain,
   I lived to feed each lustful passion's whim :
I lived to cool my hot lascivious brain
   With fragrant maidens, round of torse and limb.
The fairest beauties of fair France and Spain
   Loved me with frenzy, while my joyous hymn
With winy voice chaunted Love's languid sighs,
The coral kiss, the gleam of ravished eyes !

The white-skinned Saxon, nackered by the moon
   With long gold tresses of divinest ray,
The ebon virgin or the octaroon—
   With supple dove-like motions of dismay,
The hot-eyed maid from Venice's lagoon,
   The Russ, the Greek, or Cairo's street almée,
All who had youth and song to swell my feast,
I cherished as my happy years increased.

Erosian ecstasies from sweet-tongued girls—
   Purpled with blushes, standing statuesque,
Shading my hot brow with long ombrous curls
   Of deep gold-violet, hueful, vague, Doresque,
Demulcent bitings from sharp teeth of pearls,
   Music of sobs, of cadenced notes grotesque,
Splendors of flesh, splendors of dreams had I,
Brother I never thought that I must die !

My ferial days were sweet as were my nights,
   I spanielled to no social laws, but led—
A life of utter Spring ; of grand delights,
   Cheered by rich wines of gold, rich wines of red.

No thought of death e'er harried me by frights
     When fondling some rare beauty's tresses, spread—
In matted wantonness ;—then fears of tombs
Would fade like dreams, in revels of perfumes !

Yet churls warred with me in their wrath and zeal
     Some woman's tottering virtue to defend :
Many beneath my bitter laughing steel
     Fell on the croft, and met their timely end :
Till my day came ; and I was forced to feel
     The dastard thrust of one who called me friend :
My soul set free ; now shrink my bones and rot,
Cloistered within the horrors of this spot !

Brother, a righteous God saw fit to save
     Our inert bones from torture and from flame,
Despite the terrors of this humid grave
     'Tis better than a ceaseless Hell of shame :
I for my part no other tomb would crave,
     Tell me ! art thou contented with the same ?
The other mused awhile and murmured " yes."
God for this answer loved their souls no less.

*   *   *   *   *   *   *   *   *

SOULS OF FLOWERS.

SEE yon wondrous wild slumbrous red roses that fill
　All the air with their rare rich perfume ;
See each petal like metal that bendeth so still
In the dark shade of wood-glade and hill.
Will the white moon appear soon to thrill
　All the trembling assembling grey torrents of gloom ?

There are bright-rays and night-rays that revel in air,
　To contend and to blend with the flowers ;
The red roses in poses of fear and despair
Seem to shrink from the wink and the glare,
Of the Night's immense shadow's dense stare
　And seem sighing and dying for moonlier powers.

So the muser, the chooser of beautiful things,
　All the men born of ken and of thought ;
Rose-like slumber and number each time the moon
　　springs
Through the shrouds of Night's clouds, mist befraught,
Till its rays bless the phase of minds, taught,
　Not to hate or to wait for the song that it sings.

And each chalice, flower-palace, is in my belief
　But a hushed, fragrance-crushed poet's soul ;
For when in bloom, its perfume pervades ev'ry leaf
For its longs for a song's sweet relief,
Being haunted, Night taunted by grief,
　And it swayeth and prayeth for lights that condole.

CORDOVA.

In the vale of Andalusia,
   On the Guadalquivir's strands :
'Neath the shadows of the Sierra,
   Córdova forsaken stands.

Houses white as snow when falling
   Blend and mingle with the hue—
Purest cobalt, clear and dazzling,
   Of the Heaven's seas of blue.

Lost within a maze of lanelets,
   Alleys tortuous and steep,
Rests the wondrous Mosque-Cathedral,
   Burdened by an age of sleep.

Stern and mute with portals whitened,
   By the griefs of centuries crushed :
Stands it mourning in its grandeur
   Hopes all thwarted, memories hushed.

Yet it dreams of by-gone glories,
   When the month of Rhamadan
Lit its mammoth naves in splendor,
   When the holy rites began.

Dreams it of the nights and mornings
　　When sweet incense filled its halls,
When the golden lamps were burning
　　Eighteen hundred from its walls !

When the Caliph in the Mihrab
　　Marvel of the Moorish art,
Read the Koran's saintly precepts,
　　Dear to every Moslem heart !

When the hosts of turbaned Cadis
　　All in gorgeous robes arrayed,
With the old white-bearded Imans,
　　In the perfumed chapels prayed !

There its thousand polished pillars
　　Carved in rare and precious stone,
Jasper, lazuli and agate
　　'Neath the glare of torches shone !

Then with bodies bent towards Mecca,
　　Then the vast and mighty throng
Sang praise-pæans to Mahomet,
　　Till the Mihrab reeled with song !

Then the troupes of young Sultanas
　　Veiled in izars velvet-sleek,
Played around thy orange-gardens,
　　Dark of eye, and red of cheek.

Then the eunuchs watched and guarded
　　Toying with their sharp kandjars,
Chatting 'neath the moon's white crescent
　　'Neath the shade of Alcazars !

Then oh glorious, grand Cordova
    Didst thou hope and live and love,
Gold and verdure all around thee,
    Cloudless skies of smiles above.

Songs and revels, shouts and laughter,
    Triumphs, trophies, endless mirth,
Games and festivals succeeding—
    Others of an equal worth.

Now, fair city, all has vanished,
    Dull and desolate dost seem :
While thy great and cherished mem'ries
    Haunt thee like a phantom dream.

Through thy crooked lanes and alleys
    Search I vestiges in vain—
Of that splendid host of shadows
    Formless, that besiege my brain.

Córdova long hast thou slumbered,
    Time shall dry thy bitter tears,
God shall give thee for thy sufferings
    Life again in other spheres.

ON THE BEACH.

THE brown, red-sanded beach was still
            Dead still :
        The kisses of the wave—
Plashing upon the sea-weed, chill,
Murmurless rippled ; while the thoughts that rave
    In brains tempestuous, would blend and thrill
        All through my frame that lept—
            As stealthily I crept,
                Brave,
            Where the sad wave
Kissed the red-sanded beach so still—

She sat upon that beach, her gaze
            Fond gaze—
        Riveted on his face :
Her glance, a glance of doting praise
Was pure and loveful as was all her race,
    His arm had clasped her, and the damning rays
        Of stars on scene like this
        · Shone blandly : while my hiss
                Base,
            Echoed each embrace,
There 'neath the quiet moon-tide's blaze !

Closer crept I upon that beach
            Wild beach !
        Witness of harlots' deeds :
My wrong a lesson ached to teach,

My hands now reeked with hot and bloody beads . . .
　Each jealous hand mark well ! each hand *each, each,*
　　Then all again was still.
　　No wind, however shrill
　　　　Pleads,—
　　　When holiest creeds
　　Are severed by a woman's breach !

　　The brown, red-sanded beach was still
　　　　Dead still.
　　　The kisses of the wave—
　Plashing upon the sea-weed, chill,
Murmurless rippled ; while the thoughts that rave
　In brains tempestuous, would blend and thrill
　　　What I had done was *good*
　　　And calmly grand I stood,
　　　　Grave,
　　　Where the sad wave,
　Kissed the red-sanded beach, dead still !

LANDSCAPE OF FLESH.

In dreams I saw a monstrous, marvellous sight
　Landscape of terror : palling view of pain :
I would have shuddered in the day's broad light
　If such a fancy had disturbed my brain.
　Scene that I never can forget again
Atrocity of thought which every night
　Will haunt me with an ever-surging bane !

Within an ignored world my soul was led
  Above all darkness, high in floods of space :
Above the sun's great ball, fleck-dappled, red,
  Above the stars' domain, the comets' trace,
  Far far above and still above, my pace—
Electric, reached a planet where the dead—
  Of ages past, had found a burial place !

Trillions of bodies, Tartar, Hebrew, Greek,
  Races extinct, nations we know no more,
Profiles and faces, savage, tame, and meek,
  Humanities defunct, old tribes of yore :
  All who had perished on earth's globe before
Were congregated in this sphere unique
  By God's great will for reasons we ignore.

Was it a Heaven, second life or Hell ?
  Was it the dreaded spot where souls await
Chastisement for vile crimes, for doings fell?
  Was it the land of Sleep, or Tophet's gate ?
  I know not; but the vision I narrate
Of weird sad horror will all dreams excel :
  And God preserve my corpse from equal fate !

I roamed within a hideous land, and saw
  That ground and soil of human flesh were made
I trod on trembling bosoms hot and raw,
  At times obliged through viscera to wade.
  And, tottering onward, agonized, I prayed,
While towering rocks of flesh devoid of flaw
  Loomed 'fore my gaze in symmetry arrayed !

Down from their swaying heights great floods of tears
  White briny tears in regal tumult rolled :
A cataract of grief, all shed in years
  Forever gone : drops precious as new gold,
  Compelled to dash and plash in torrents cold
Over those fleshful cliffs in doomèd spheres
  Awful to think of—hideous to behold !

Beyond, I saw a vast rage-fuming sea—
  Of crimson bloods : thick waves with ceaseless roar
Broke with a brutal savageness of glee
  Upon a beach of human nail—a shore
  Besprent with jaggèd teeth, grim shells, all sore,
Gnashing a hymn of ivory melody,
  Timed by the deep swift bubbling tides of gore !

A half-light reigned, above, great lurid skies
  Of burnished skin, shone sleekly on the scene :
Leagues upon leagues, grand, vast, while staring eyes
  Of colors two, in millions, blue and green
  Shed a pale glassy flicker to survene
And lume the flesh-crags or to harmonize
  With tints cadaverous that served as screen !

Huge pools of bile and marrow here and there,
  Nourished dwarfed trees with solid trunks of bone,
While from their boughs hung leaves of fibrous hair
  Willowy, gnarly, and all groundward prone :
  Some seemed the tresses of a hag or crone
Others the silkier locks of maidens fair,
  All blooming in this hybrid nameless zone !

Gazing stood I with pain and wonder mute,
　　Striving to shun the skin-sky's sullen light:
Nescient and cowed, but curious as a brute
　　I could not yet conceive the awful sight.
　　Nor feel the power of God's most boundless might,
A will of iron which nothing could refute
　　Forced me to long for fleshless air and night.

No soul, no sound, no welcome step was heard
　　Save time to time a ghost-wail from the sky,
Trilled from the hoarse throat of a weird odd bird—
　　Which featherless and gaunt soared moaning by,
　　I saw it swoop to clutch a wart, then fly—
Over the long hair branches which it stirred,
　　Then dive into the blood sea with a sigh. . . .

Night's ash veil fell, terrific, solemn gloom
　　Aroused me: while the eye-stars blinked and blazed:
Then woke to me the grandeur of this tomb
　　Its horrid splendors, wild, sublime, bedazed
　　My fear-chilled heart, as sank I down amazed
Musing on wicked worlds I left—their doom
　　Inevitably fatal—till I crazed. . . .

The forms and faces that I loved on earth
　　Must they when dead in such a planet dwell?
Must lips I prized when once alert with mirth
　　Come also to this livid horrid Hell?
　　Must righteous souls be damned and doomed as well
Is there no difference in a mortal's worth?
　　No! no! I see that ghastly ocean swell. . . .

Its waves rise higher, God ! its red sprays burst
   Roughly upon the flesh-cliffs far below,
Each soul that dies on earth is here accursed :
   New eyes must shine here, and new blood must flow,
   Fresh corpses and fresh bones new worlds bestow
To quench this howling ocean's sateless thirst,
   My place with others has been marked I know !

Reeking with pain, I struggled on and fled,—
   Odors of clotted blood pursued my sense :
Round, round the hateful spot with dizzy head
   I rushed, and in my agonies intense,
   Dashed through the tear-falls and their brine-mist
     dense
On ! on ! I living in a land of dead !
   Till worn I woke :—'twas but a dream immense ! . . .

THE END.